To Dori

Unlocking Pandora's Box

by

Kendall Jaye

To all our stories together
as yet unwritten

Kendall Jaye

LSP
After Dark

"Jay"

First Edition

Editing, Formatting, & Cover Design by:
LSP After Dark

Disclaimer

As with all factual or actual, or fantasy stories, any connection with any living or dead person or persons is purely accidental and was never intended to harm anyone, and was purely coincidental and unintentional. And no animals were harmed in the writing of any of these stories.

ISBN-13: **978-1979587990**

ISBN-10: **197958799X**

PUBLISHED BY **LSP AFTER DARK**

www.lspafterdark.com

Printed in the United States of America

Dedication

To my wife, my lover, my best friend. Thank you for your support as well as participation. Wow! What a ride! Grow old with me. The best is yet to be! I love you!

To the ones who have in one way or another contributed to the stories. Thank you!

May we have many more stories and adventures worthy of writing about!

To the paradise, we call home. What a happy place! Thank you for your visionary thoughts to bring this to ... I was going to say "completion," but it is only the beginning of this roller coaster ride we call life.

To the future and beyond!

Table of Contents

Chapter One

When In Rome

My favorite sight is to see my hot wife's hand encircling another man's cock with her engagement and wedding rings sparkling as she takes him in her mouth, working his shaft. She knows how much I love that sight, and looks over at me smiling as I watch the erotic scene. I am the luckiest man in the world to have a wife who lets me share her with other men.

It all started four years ago when we were on our first European holiday in Rome, a sort of delayed honeymoon a year after we married. On our last day, Judi and I were having lunch in a very nice restaurant just across the square from our hotel. It was a warm May afternoon and we happily drank our wine and enjoyed the Roman scene unfolding around us.

As lunch progressed, I realized that Judi kept looking over my shoulder and was becoming increasingly distracted. Occasionally she would lower her eyes coyly and smile.

"What's going on over my shoulder?" I asked.

"I can't believe the cheek of these Italian men! There's a good looking guy a few tables away flirting with me! He can see I am with you. He's shameless."

"Do you think he knows you are married?"

"Of course! Look at my rings sparkling in the sun!" "Describe him to me and tell me what he's doing!"

Judi told me he was handsome and very well dressed, drinking a small carafe of white wine. Occasionally he would blow her a kiss or put his fingers to his lips and make a gesture expressing how beautiful she was. A couple of times he had winked at her.

As she was describing all this, I could see she was getting flustered and blushing, and I began to realize she was enjoying the attention.

But, suddenly, evil thoughts came into my mind, another man flirting with Judi was also turning me on.

"Why don't you flirt back and surprise him?" I asked, "He probably gets a kick out of the fact you are married."

"I couldn't do that!" exclaimed Judi, surprised, but giggling at the idea.

"Of course you can. As they say, 'When in Rome' ..."

Judi thought about it for a few moments and looked away across the square. I thought she was going to change the subject, but she surprised me.

"What should I do?" she asked simply, looking at me with a naughty twinkle in her eye.

"Your dress was very short. Why don't you open your legs and see if he notices!"

"I can't believe you want me to flash another man, you dirty bastard! I'm your wife!"

Exactly, I thought privately to myself. That's the whole point. I want to show my wife to another guy, who I haven't even seen yet!

"Only do it if you want to," I said, nonchalantly. "It's not a dare." I knew Judi would take it as a dare!

With barely a second of hesitation, Judi changed position on her chair and uncrossed her legs. Then she slid forwards a little, pushing up her skirt still higher and opened her legs. Finally she flashed a big smile over my shoulder to her admirer and then looked back into my eyes.

"Satisfied?" she inquired triumphantly, thinking it was the end of it, but I had other ideas.

"I'm sure I will be later. Right now I just want to know what happens next!"

Judi tried to stare me down and not look over to her Latin beau. I could see she was desperate to gauge his reaction. I raised an eyebrow questioningly and she flinched, looking back towards him.

"If you want to know, he is looking right between my legs and blowing me kisses towards my pussy!"

I could feel my cock growing hard. I wanted Judi to go further, much further.

"Why don't you unbutton the top of your sun dress? Let him see a bit more of your amazing breasts!"

"He's going to think I'm trying to seduce him!"

I took my chance. "Would you like to?" I asked, staring deep into Judi's eyes. I could see her hesitating long enough to know she was pondering the implications of my question. She was getting flushed. But soon I had my answer.

"It's getting hot out here," said Judi, winking at me as she started to unbutton her dress down to the middle of her cleavage.

"VERY hot!" I exclaimed. "Is your lover watching you?"

"He's NOT my lover, and yes, he is watching me!"

"Then I'm sure he WANTS to be your lover," I goaded.

"Maybe not," said Judi, sounding disappointed. He's called over the waiter and I think he's asked for the bill."

"What a shame. I was beginning to get turned on watching you seduce a total stranger."

"You dirty bastard!"

We need not have worried about her man going, because in a few minutes a bottle of ice-cold white wine arrived and the waiter explained, "The gentleman over there says you have a very beautiful wife, and he would like to buy you both some wine to help you enjoy Rome."

He certainly was confident!

The waiter poured our wine, and I turned to toast him with Judi, raising our glasses in thanks. He put the tips of his fingers to his lips and gestured a kiss. He called out to me, standing and raising his glass.

"You have a very sexy wife mister! Be careful or she will want to explore new passions in Rome! I know about these things!"

Judi and I sat there a little stunned. The sexual tension was electric.

"What do we do next?" Judi asked. "I hope he doesn't expect to come over here and join us?"

"Would that be a bad thing?" "I'm too embarrassed!"

"That's not what I asked."

"But I've been showing myself off to him. If we invite him over, we are just encouraging him."

"Encouraging him to do what?"

Judi blushed, "To have sex with me, of course. That's what he wants."

"You really think it would go that far?" I asked, in my heart begging Judi to say yes.

"If I let him."

"I don't mind if you let it happen."

Judi looked at me quizzically, trying to work out how I really felt. I took her hand and pulled it to the raging hard-on in my pants. She let out a little gasp when she realized that I wanted her to go ahead.

"I mean it. I don't mind. In fact, I would like you to have an Italian lover!"

"Oh my God, this is all happening too fast, and I am getting so horny!" she confessed.

"So, is that a yes?" There was a long pause.

"Yes. Invite him over. I'm going to the restroom to get my head straight. If I sit in this seat when I come back it means I am willing to try it. If I sit in another place, then you have to help me get out of here because I'm not going to let it happen. Okay? You agree?"

"Yes, of course, I agree. It should only happen if you want it!"

With that, Judi stood up and started to walk to the restroom.

When she arrived at her admirer's table, she paused to thank him again for his hospitality, and he stood up, taking her hand, which he kissed, and then held on to her arm, caressing it while they spoke.

Then she was gone and I called the man over, Marco, as he introduced himself. He was warm and gracious as he sat down at our table, paying Judi and me many compliments, and saying how Rome at this time of year always made sexy young women blossom and think of love.

As we waited for Judi to return, Marco asked me directly if I would mind if he made love to my wife. I said I would be perfectly happy if it was what she wanted. I also explained that I wanted to be there to watch and participate, which seemed to please Marco.

"Ah, so you are a sexy man who wants to see his wife have pleasure with another. For me this is always the most exciting!"

I was wondering how many times he had successfully fucked other men's wives, when Judi arrived back. We both stood to greet her and she hovered there while I introduced her to Marco. He kissed her on both cheeks in the Italian way and graciously pulled out the chair where she had sat before.

My heart started pounding. She would have to walk around Marco to get to the other chair, so she was almost trapped. Judi looked at me with a devilish grin. "What the heck! When in Rome ..." and she sat down in the 'yes' chair. I was ecstatic!

Marco immediately started paying her unreasonable amounts of attention. He was nevertheless smooth and accomplished as he made Judi relax. Frequently he took her hand and stroked her inner forearm. Another bottle of wine was ordered, and by now we were all very relaxed. I noticed Marco eying Judi's free hanging breasts, and realized she had removed her bra in the restroom. Judi made sure her short dress was riding high and Marco was copping a look whenever he could.

As we reached the end of the wine Judi announced she had had enough to drink and should probably have a lie down. I suggested we walk across the square to our hotel.

"Shall we invite Marco to join us?" I asked.

Judi simply opened her purse and pulled out her tiny panties, dropping them on the table. She had been showing her naked pussy to Marco all this time!

"Finally!" she sighed, "I have been ready for over an hour. Now I am going to need a really good fuck, so I hope you two are up for it!"

Judi leaned forward and flung her arms around Marco's neck and gave him a full kiss. Then she turned to me with eyes heavy with lust. "I want this so much!"

Marco explained that the bill was already taken care of, and we just got up and crossed the square.

Marco's arm around Judi's waist and I was holding her hand.

As soon as we were in our hotel room the action started. Judi and Marco stood at the end of the bed kissing passionately, while I watched. He paid special attention to her neck and I could see her melting into his arms. She unbuttoned his shirt and kissed his hairy chest. Then Marco lifted her dress over her head and revealed her exquisite naked body. His hands were expert and Judi completely surrendered to his touch. She looked over to where I was undressing and smiled when she saw my massive hard on. She turned to Marco and said she wanted him naked too.

Judi laid back on the bed, and I stepped over to kiss her fully on the mouth while Marco completed undressing.

"I want to watch you enjoy him first," I whispered into her ear, "is that okay?"

"As long as you join in soon. I want to feel two men making love to me at the same time. That's my fantasy!" I had never known that.

"Then let's make it come true, my darling!" I kissed her again and Marco joined her on the bed.

I stepped back and Judi rolled into Marco's arms. I was rewarded with the most erotic image of my young beautiful wife giving herself to another man. He kissed and caressed her in a way that I could tell he was an experienced lover. He was both strong and gentle at the same time.

Judi pushed Marco onto his back and began to kiss down his chest towards his cock. He was well sized, and perhaps a little longer than me, but slightly thinner. As the afternoon sun streamed onto the two lovers, I watched Judi take Marco's cock and wrap her hand around it, her wedding and engagement rings catching the sunlight and sparkling to tell me I was watching my bride. At that second, as her lips opened and she welcomed his cock tip into her warm mouth, I took a mental picture and knew that I would want to see that image time and time again.

Marco pulled Judi's leg over his head so they were in the sixty nine position. I know how beautiful her sweet pussy tastes, and it thrilled me to see Marco drinking her nectar. He must have been good because very soon she was moaning onto his cock and I could see her rhythm was faltering as she had her first wrenching orgasm.

Judi flopped off Marco and lay panting on her back. Before she had time to recover Marco was touching her inflamed pussy and taking position between her legs. Judi motioned for me to join them on the bed.

"Come over here, darling. I want you with me for this."

I knelt on the bed next to her and took her hand, looking lovingly into her eyes. A thousand meanings were exchanged in that second. We both knew this was exactly what we wanted.

Marco's cock was now probing the folds of her pussy. He hesitated for a second as if to seek my permission, which I didn't need to give him, really. I just nodded and he pushed his cock into my wife as she let out a little whimpering moan. It was done. Another man was in her. I was in ecstasy and so was Judi!

With each deep thrust, Judi would let out a sigh of pleasure. I leaned forwards and locked my mouth on hers. Her hot gasping breath made our kiss all the more exciting as I felt her getting high on Marco's cock. We stayed like that for a while until I could sense she was getting close to cumming. Then I pulled away a little.

Judi was looking intently at Marco now, concentrating on her lover.

"Oh, yes, that's it. Oh! Just like that. Oh, that's SO good!"

Judi wrapped her legs behind Marco, drawing him deeper into her pussy. She looked up at me, her eyes now hooded with absolute lust. She loved this more than I could have ever hoped. It seemed quite natural and perfect for her to be fucking another man right here in front of me.

I recognized the sounds my wife makes as she approaches orgasm, little yelping gasps growing into loud guttural moans. Her eyes closed, and she threw back her head as she always does. And then the shuddering convulsions started as my wife began to cum on Marco's cock, her hand gripping mine tightly with each spasm.

Judi's orgasm seemed to trigger Marco's too, and with gasps of 'bellissima,' he unloaded into my wife's hot welcoming womb. Judi's eyes flashed open when she felt his hot gushes and a wicked grin formed. She winked at me and began to laugh happily as the emotion overwhelmed her. She reached up and pulled Marco down so they could kiss.

"You are a wonderful lover, Marco!" she complimented him, between tender kisses. Marco and I took turns kissing her and then the erotic situation began to develop. Marco pulled out of Judi, his cock slimy and dripping with their combined juices.

"Bring that beautiful cock up here, so I can clean you off," commanded Judi. She grabbed a couple of pillows to help lift her head, and Marco knelt in front of her face, slipping his cock into her waiting mouth. I took up position between her legs and slipped a finger into her used pussy, which was burning hot. I could feel a huge volume of Marco's cum and without hesitating I leaned forwards so I could inspect Judi's puffy box. From her position. sucking Marco, Judi could see my face between her legs. She knew what was coming next! I withdrew my finger and sucked Marco's cum off it, surprised how good it tasted. That was all the encouragement I needed and soon I was lapping at Judi's hole and drinking in Marco's cum. Her pussy was already very sensitive and it wasn't long before she came again, pushing more of his cum into my mouth with each contraction.

I stopped sucking her and could see that Marco's cock was getting hard in her mouth. I started to turn Judi over and instantly she knew what I wanted, positioning herself on all fours with Marco's cock in her mouth.

Then it was my turn to thrust into my wife, knowing I was second in line for her juicy snatch today. I rammed her hard, driving her mouth onto Marco's cock. It was so hot to turn my wife into a cock sandwich! After all the waiting, I didn't last long, and soon I was pumping into her willing pussy, more cum than I could ever remember.

When I had finished, I turned around and flopped down in the bed, so my head was just on the edge. Judi knows how much I like sixty nine to finish our sessions and she quickly understood what I wanted. She moved down the bed and straddled my face, her knees just on the edge of the bed. Marco was a bit unsure of the plan, so Judi told him. "Fuck me from behind while he eats me." Then Judi dropped forwards and took my recovering cock in her mouth.

Marco didn't hesitate, and in a few seconds his now hard cock appeared just above my face and he slid into Judi, his pungent hairy balls resting on my nose. I was inches away from his cock as he drove into her, forcing my own cum to drip out of her slot into my waiting mouth. This is probably my favorite position because I can really witness another man's cock in my wife so close up.

Marco pounded away for a long time, and, between his thrusts and my licking, we brought Judi to three more orgasms before he finally came. I loved the moment when his ball sack contracted and I could feel him pumping into her. As his shrinking cock withdrew, it flopped for a moment onto my lips and left a trail of cum across my face.

With that I exploded into Judi's mouth. We took a short break and took turns to visit the bathroom. When I came back, Judi was already straddling Marco's cock, and this time they were enjoying a slow loving session. Outside the sun was nearly gone, and the room had taken on a more subdued feel. I slipped on a robe and sat back in a chair to watch my wife make tender love to another man, knowing that our life would never be the same again.

Marco kept telling Judi how beautiful and sexy she was. She in turn told him he was a great lover and how exciting it had been to have her first threesome with him.

When eventually they had finished, Marco excused himself and said it was time to leave. When he had gone I joined my lovely wife in the bed. We cuddled and kissed, touching each other and discussed what just happened.

"Are you okay with what we just did?" I asked.

"What do you think?" laughed Judi, smiling broadly, "I have never come so much in my life and I got to live out my dirtiest fantasy for the first time!"

"It was my fantasy too," I confessed. "I'm sorry I never told you before. I thought you would be mad at me."

She was surprised, but we both agreed it had worked out just fine, and it had been a perfect way to discover we both shared similar desires.

"What was your favorite moment?" asked Judi.

"When you took his cock in your hand for the first time. The sun made your engagement and wedding rings sparkle, and it made it even more erotic knowing you are my wife and I was watching you enjoy another man. I will always remember that moment!"

"Well, it's good to know what you like to watch. I will remember to put on a good show with my ring hand if this ever happens again."

"What was your favorite moment, darling?"

"When you kissed me as he first entered me. I felt we were doing this together. I was so in love with you at that moment ..." she hesitated and then gave a quick giggle, "And all the sex of course. That was the best sex ever!"

"Would you do it again, if there is an opportunity?"

"If we do it together again, if we are both happy with the situation, then yes!"

"I hoped you would say that," I said, kissing my sexy wife and slipping my finger into her pussy. "Oh, it feels like you still have a lot of Marco's cum in here. I hope you're not keeping it to yourself?"

"Not at all!" exclaimed Judi, opening her legs as an invitation. "I intend to make my pussy the cup from which you drink many men's cum! So you may as well get used to it!"

I have. Over the last four years I have supped the cum of seventeen men from Judi's pussy. I have watched her ring fingers encircle every one of their cocks, and I have several photos now in our growing collection of erotic memories.

Really, I am the most happily married man, I know!

Chapter Two

The Joy of Sharing My Wife With Others

There really is no other feeling that matches what it's like to be lying in bed next to your naked wife, having caressed her, kissed her and told her how much I loved her. And she responds likewise, as she lays on her back with her body, expressing how much she needed raw, naughty almost primitive sexual satisfaction.

The man we have both agreed to share her with was in bed with us and eager to make hot, naughty love to her. She wanted him, and willingly, eagerly spread her legs and used her hands to guide his naked, moist and warm body into position between her open legs to take her.

Seeing his erect, excited throbbing cock first touch my beautiful wife's pussy lips, wetting the head of his cock from her wetness, preparing to enter her as she pulled her knees up higher to open herself for him to take her as she freely gave us both the most precious, intimate gift she has to give to us. Then seeing him gently push the tip of his cock finding my wife's wet lips, both of their bodies then lined up to join together. I love seeing her shift her hips upward slightly to welcome his cock into her.

As he pushed past her tight wet opening, her legs raised a little to allow him to slip deep into her craving cunt. Then I heard my wife make sudden little cries and moans, and even though part of my mind rebelled at the thought of her so thoroughly enjoying his cock slip into her, I know that the sounds she was making means that the head of his cock had entered her and she loved how he was making her feel. Their bodies began moving in rhythm with each other, and I admired the sexy curve of my wife's smooth thighs spread wide for his naked body to enjoy. I shifted around to the side of the bed to watch them pause for a passionate kiss as his cock was buried deeply inside her. Her eyes closed, her tongue feeling the sensations of touching and tasting his as they enjoy each other's bodies while they fuck.

I too held her head and lovingly kissed her and whispered in her ear, "I love you, let yourself go and enjoy," as her beautiful breasts bounced each time he thrust into her. With each thrust, the clenching of his ass cheeks as he buried his erect cock in her sweet pussy, I knew the pleasure his throbbing cock was giving her, and her reaction to him confirmed this as an indisputable fact. I can tell when she first started to feel her orgasm beginning by the way she moaned, holding his hips, controlling his thrusts to maximize her climax and pleasure. I could also tell from his moans and the way his ass cheeks were tensing as he thrust his cock deeply into her, that he loved the feeling of pleasure and relief as he felt his cum being involuntarily squirted through his cock deeply inside her pussy.

He laid on top of her, supporting himself on his elbows, gently kissing her as they enjoyed the afterglow of their mutual orgasm. After a few more minutes of kissing and small gentle movements, her pussy was sounding and smelling of being so soaking wet from his cum and her love juices, his exhausted cock, then half of its erect size, slipped out of her. As he rolled off of her, I eagerly rushed to take his place. I was so excited for the opportunity to make love to her and fill her freshly fucked pussy with my highly excited, hard throbbing cock. I slid in with ease, as her warm cunt is full of his warm slippery cum and her love fluids.

That is the intense pleasure I get from having my wife share her wonderful body and pussy with another man we both connect with, and the one whom she desires, and the one who desires her so much. I feel no jealousy as our love is very strong. We both receive immense pleasure from sharing with another man our most intimate desires that we crave to satisfy. I love watching her in the throes of passion and the feel of making love to her, and enjoying her freshly fucked pussy is beyond describing in words. The combination of all our love of passionate sex combined is simply out of this world. There are just no words that can describe the feelings that run through my mind and body when watching another man help me to take my wife's mind, as well as her body to this higher and intense level of pleasure.

Watching and caressing her as she trembles with wave after wave of satisfying sexual pleasure pleases me as well as her. My sexual arousal is at the very highest level, every little sound she makes in her sexual pleasure, every little move she makes to impale that hard throbbing cock deeper into her moist warm cunt, every thrust he makes, all these things and many more, brings so much more pleasure to us both than just my cock filling her wonderful pussy. In sharing my wife with other men, my wife and I can both be taken to sexual heights we can never achieve on our own.

Having the right partner to join us is of prime importance. One who is sensitive to her needs foremost, and secondary to mine or his own. After all, we invited him to share.

Chapter Three

First Time

It finally happened! We got together and hit it off. As Judi was licking her pussy, you were eating Judi's pussy, and I was sucking your cock getting it ready to go into Judi so I could have a fresh cream pie. Judi is quite good at eating pussy and this caused her to cum huge and drench Judi's face. I then placed my achingly hard cock at the entrance to her pussy and pressed slowly into the very bottom. It was warm and juicy. You slid your hard cock into Judi at the same time. It didn't take long to finish at that pace. As you came, Judi did also. Then we followed shortly after that. You had a fresh cream pie as was evidenced in the photos we took, and so did I.

Rhonda was sitting on your cock, and Judi was sitting on your face, facing each other. As they kissed each other, I was taking photos and movies to enjoy later. When it became too painful to watch, I placed my cock between both of their lips and slid it back and forth. When I came, they let it shoot in your mouth and then took turns licking it off as I ate each one of them from behind. I then sucked your cock hard while I cleaned Rhonda's juices off. Judi climbed on your big hard cock and began to ride while I ate her, and Rhonda ate me out from behind. I sucked on your nuts and licked your crack as Judi humped your cock. As you said you were coming, Rhonda pulled your cock out, and Judi and her shared the load as you and I watched and took photos and videos. I cleaned you up and you cleaned me up.

I stripped Judi and laid her on my coffee table. I then straddled her on the table and I put my cock on her chest, and then pushed her big tits together and started fucking them. Rhonda spread Judi's legs and started licking her pussy. You were standing in front of me so I could lean forward and take your cock in my mouth. As we continued this arrangement, you and I began to cum. We both came on Judi's face and tits, and got Rhonda to kiss it off. We smeared the cum around as they kissed.

"How about you slowly take my wife's clothing off, licking and sucking as you go? I asked, "I will do the same to your wife. When they are stripped they will take our clothing off, licking and sucking as they go. When your cock is nice and hard, Rhonda will sit you down on a chair and sit on your cock with her back to you. I will kneel in front of her and lick her clit while your cock slides in and out an inch away."

"Your wife will be sucking my cock while lying on her side. As I lick Rhonda's pussy, I will be sliding my tongue up and down your cock as it slides around in that pussy. Every now and then I'll pull it out, suck it for a while, and put it back in. I'll then change places with your wife. She can sit on my face while she licks Rhonda's clit and sucks your cock. I'll be playing with my cock as I lick your wife's pussy. When we get ready to cum, well, then we will decide where or who gets the juice." Those were some of the words that day, words I will never forget!

Judi and Rhonda were doing 69 on the edge of the bed. You and I were also doing 69 beside them. The girls had their free hands around the base of our cocks very tightly to making our cock swell even more. When we started getting close, we got up and you took Rhonda and I took Judi. They continued to suck each other while we put our cocks in their pussies. We then put them on their sides so we could see each other fuck the other's wife.

This was written for her, "We would meet for dinner. I am to do the cooking. As I prepare the meal, we engage in small talk sipping on wine. We do not talk sex, but all three know that is the underlying tension. We converse on a variety of topics. During dinner we toast each other and toast to an enjoyable evening with each of us having an idea of how the evening will go. But we do not express it."

After dinner, we moved to the sofa. We continued to drink wine and talk. You were sitting in the middle. During the conversation, without anyone saying what to do, I started unbuttoning your blouse. Your breasts were exposed, held within your bra. Jerry and I then started rubbing your breasts through your bra. I then removed the blouse. I reached behind you and undid your bra strap, showing us your beautiful breasts. We then started sucking on your breasts, and started sucking and gently biting on your nipples. You started to moan with pleasure.

Jerry then reached down under your skirt and rubbed your nectar of sweetness. You were not wearing underwear. He felt how wet you had become. He told me! I then reached under your skirt. You were smooth and very wet. In inserted my finger, while Jerry and I continued to lick and suck your nipples. I gently rubbed inside you. You moaned again. I removed my finger and put it in my mouth to taste your sweetness. Jerry removed your skirt allowing he and I to view your beautiful pussy.

I could not resist, and had to start licking on it. I licked and sucked on your clit while Jerry continued to feel and suck on your breasts. Your pussy got wetter with anticipation of what soon was coming. While I licked your clit, I inserted my finger, and you moaned again.

You felt the pleasure of having two men stimulate you.

I continued to suck and lick on you, while Jerry removed his clothes. His dick had become hard from seeing his wife enjoy so much pleasure. You then took Jerry's hard dick in your mouth. He moaned with pleasure as you lick, and your tongue made his dick even harder. I stopped licking on you to watch you give him so much pleasure. My dick got hard watching the incredible way you sucked his dick and played with his balls.

I could stand it no longer. I too quickly removed my clothes. You then saw my dick standing up from the excitement of what I have enjoyed and what I was seeing. You then reached out and grabbed my dick. You started stroking it. I had to resist cumming. You then took my dick in your mouth while holding on to Jerry's dick. For the first time I felt the incredible warmth of your mouth on my dick. I watched you stroke Jerry's dick while you sucked mine. The feeling made me lightheaded. It was hard not to cum.

Jerry then suggested that we retire to the bedroom. I was more than willing, as I thought about how good your wet and hot nectar of sweetness would feel around my dick. In the bedroom, Jerry pulled back the spread and we both gently put you on the cool sheets. Jerry now had to taste your juices. I watched him between your legs. I could only see the back of his head, but from your cries I knew what he was doing, and that he was giving you pleasure. I then brought my dick near your mouth, and you started sucking on it while Jerry continued to enjoy your sweetness.

Jerry stopped, and turned you over. I missed the warmth of your mouth on my dick. He then entered you from behind. I sat in front of you while his dick slowly at first, then faster, entered you. He told me how good it was. He was excited. You started saying how good it felt to have him fucking you. You told me how good his dick felt in your pussy. Your dirty talk excited me even more. I was ready to explode!

Jerry then removed himself from you. Without saying a word I knew that it was time for me to know the pleasure of being in you. Jerry watched me enter your pussy. He got excited watching his wife being fucked by another man. He started to play with his dick. You told him not to cum, that you wanted it all from both of us.

I pulled out and laid on the bed, on my back. You mounted me. Jerry was beside you and you sucked on his dick. The sensation of having a dick in your pussy and another in your mouth was too much. You came. I could feel your pussy tightening around my dick as you came. I could see you sucking on Jerry's dick. From his face I knew he was excited and about to cum. The visual sensation was too much for me. I came in your pussy. You could feel the hot cum shooting inside you. Jerry too got excited when I came knowing that his wife had another man cumming inside her. He could hold no longer. He said he was cumming. I watched you get excited with the anticipation of tasting his cum. He came in your mouth. He slowly pulled out and I could see his cum slowly dripping out of the corners of your mouth. We were all very satisfied. Jerry and I then laid down with you and held on to you while we thought about the pleasure we all shared.

We relaxed together. We talked very little for a while. We then talked about how good it was. We started planning our next encounter. I told you that next time I would bring a friend for you and Jerry to enjoy.

Chapter Four

Sharing My Wife

This writing is an attempt to explain my feelings from sharing my wife with other men. Once again, as I mentioned in a previous chapter, there are no other feelings that match what it is like to see your wife on her back, her arms flung over her head, spreading her thighs as another man moves into position to fuck her, his body taking the place of yours. I can't help revisiting the intense feelings that these moments generated, seeing his hard throbbing cock next to my wife's pussy as she pulls her knees back to open herself to him, watching as he settles his weight down onto her, seeing her hands embracing him. Then seeing him push forward, the tip of his cock finding my wife's pussy lips, both of their bodies lined up to join, is ecstasy, watching as their hips shift slightly, his pushing down as her legs rise in the air.

Then I hear my wife make a little cry and moan, and even though part of my mind rebels at the thought, I know that the sounds she is making means the head of his cock has entered her. I watch with great anticipation as he shoves the full length of his cock fully in to her deepest parts. Their bodies begin to move in rhythm, and I admire the curve of my wife's smooth thighs against his hips. I shift around to the other side of the bed to watch them kiss, her eyes closed, her tongue searching for his, and then I look closely between their legs to see the shaft of his cock spreading her pussy lips, then seeing his balls swinging as he pulls his cock part way out then shoves it all the way in again. With each thrust, the clenching of his ass as he buries his stiff cock in her wonderful pussy, I know exactly what he is feeling, as my wife's pussy grips his penis, as I also know the feeling his throbbing cock gives her moist and warm pussy. I know as she reaches orgasm by the way her toes curl and she moans slightly.

As he cums in her and rolls off of her, I rush to fill her freshly fucked pussy with my own throbbing cock. I slide in with ease as her warm pussy is full of his cum and her fluids. This is the pleasure I get from having my wife share her wonderful pussy with another man. I feel no jealousy as our love is very strong for each other. We both receive immense pleasure from another man shoving his strong and hard cock into her juicy pussy. I love watching her in the throes of passion as I am very voyeuristic, and the feel and smells of her freshly fucked pussy is beyond description. I enjoy a pussy full of love wine. The combination of all our sex fluids is out of this world!

There are just no words that can describe the feelings that run through my body, watching another man doing many wonderful things to my wife's body taking her to higher and higher levels of pleasure. My body trembles with wave after wave of sexual pleasure that is almost as intense as a full-blown ejaculation orgasm. At times I can barely stand. My sexual arousal is at its highest level when listening to every little sound she makes in her sexual pleasure center as she makes adjustments to impale that hard and throbbing cock even deeper into her moist pussy. Every thrust he makes and all these things, and many more, bring so much pleasure to me and them than just my cock filling her wonderful pussy.

In sharing my wife with other men, my wife and I can both be taken to sexual heights we can never achieve on our own. Having the right partner to join us is of the utmost importance. One who is sensitive to her needs first, and then his and mine. We have had some one night stands, and some that were stopped before going very far, due to his attitude or actions. Yes, she fucks other men. No, she is not a slut. She shares her body to please us, and, if I asked her to stop she would immediately.

I willing share those adventures we've had with you, so that you too can ponder what it must be like, and what you too can experience once you realize that letting go of old, preconceived notions regarding sex can bring incredible moments of intense delight.

Chapter Five

Once Upon A Time

This story started as all do, once upon a time. We met a couple who wanted to meet with us to see if we were compatible with them for a friends with benefit relation. After the lunch we decided with our usual signal with each other to take it further with the couple. We went to our house and began by all four of us in the same bed. We began petting each other's spouses, and started undressing and kissing each part as it was uncovered. She was soft and blonde, and passionate with me. I could hear the other guy with my wife as she began to moan her approval of what he was doing. I know my wife's sounds and enjoy hearing her being passionate with another man.

I watched him position himself between her legs and prepare to enter her. I could hear her gasp and could tell he had made contact with her pussy. I watched her face as he went deeper, and then held himself still so she could adjust to his size. She signaled it was all right to continue as she started rotating her hips and thrusting against his hips to get him to continue fucking her.

His wife became impatient with me being distracted, and grabbed me by my ears, pulling me back into her pussy so she could continue enjoying what I was doing. Soon, it became a competition to see who could make the women sigh and squeal and moan the loudest.

My wife, being the most passionate woman I have ever met, was without a doubt the winner as she screamed and squirted and soaked his cock and balls, and belly and legs. This was his first time with a squirter, and he was delighted and asked for more. Needlessly to say she began to give him an endless stream, as once she starts she can go on forever until she drains all she has.

As I am not circumcised, and he was, she was enjoying the difference, as his wife was enjoying my extra bit of skin, as she had never been with a man who was not circumcised. After I had made his wife cum until she said, "zebra," which was our safe word, I then let her turn to watch her husband and my wife fuck as she began to give me oral to make me harder, if possible. The sights and sounds and smells were so exciting for me, as I am a voyeur and thrive on smells and taste being very tactile. It was a delight!

When she started tasting my precum, she said it was time to fuck. She nimbly swung around in the bed so she was laying crossways, with her ass at the edge. I stepped between her thighs, as this is one of my favorite positions, and placed the head of my cock between her lips. I stroked up and down to wet the head of my cock, and then slowly pushed into her pussy as she gasped and gripped my arms. When I bottomed out, I held still and let her adjust to my size. Soon she started whimpering and moving her hips side to side, so I knew she was ready for the ride. I pulled almost out and slowly went back in again.

She was a very small woman, and each time I went deep, I had to be careful as I hit bottom every time, and she would gasp as she had not felt a cock do that before. The look on her face was a look of surprise and excitement, to feel a cock where one had never been before. With that I began to thrust with more speed and she slowly opened up and I could push harder, which I love to do, as I thrust strongly in that position. She began to cum, and I had to watch her closely as she was quiet and I could only tell by her expression and feel as she tightened up.

I could hear my wife and her husband as they continued to fuck, and I saw his wife reach for my wife's hand, and they grasped each other tightly. He was getting ready to cum, and my wife was encouraging him to fuck her good, and fill her up so she could clean him out. That made him immediately cum with a moan. She said excitedly for me to let her up so she could clean his cock and my wife's pussy. She scrambled over and took his cock when it came out of my wife, and began quickly sucking and licking all of the juices off his cock while moaning the whole time. She then had her husband move so she could take his place on her hands and knees and then told me to fuck her from behind while she cleaned my wife up. I jumped behind her and thrust into her in almost the same motion.

She was licking my wife, which caused her to squirt again, and she began cumming a lot herself in excitement. The extra pressure when she came around my cock proved to be more than I could stand, and I came in buckets inside her, and my wife said she had to have that and not to waste it. They both moved to a sixty nine position and proceeded to clean each other up as her husband and I watched as our cocks revived.

The next session will have to be another chapter I suppose.

Chapter Six

Saint Marten

Well, there was the time that we were in the Caribbean island of Saint Marten. We had a individual house on a nude beach on the French side of the island. We laid around all day nude and got turned on by the sun and atmosphere, and got really horny, then would have hot sex every night. The atmosphere was quiet and in general the people stayed to themselves.

One evening the resort had a wine and cheese social, and we attended. We met a couple from New York, and talked awhile and drank some wine. As the evening progressed, I found myself talking to the wife of the other couple, and my wife was carrying on a conversation with the husband. I do not remember how the conversation got started, but the wife, whose name was TJ, started telling me how she and her girlfriend one night surprised their husbands with a little dirty dancing and some suggestive touching of each other. They thought it would be funny to see the looks on their husband's faces. As it turned out, they were surprised at how turned on their husbands got, and decided to start to strip each other. She finished by telling me that the guys got so turned on that the girls continued on until the they were naked and pleasuring each other. She said that it was a huge turn-on for the guys.

I mentioned that my wife had always wondered what it would be like with another woman, but had never been with another woman before. She looked at me and asked would my wife like to be with her. I suggested that she ask Judi and find out.

Later that evening the two women walked off down the beach talking, and, when my wife returned, she told me that we were going to go to this other couple's apartment the next night. Later that evening I asked my wife what she was talking about with TJ, and she told me that TJ had told her of our conversation, and wondered if she would like to get together with her while the guys watched. My wife had agreed.

The next night we went to their place and I wondered how the evening was going to go, but could not have imagined what would really transpire. After some wine and some dinner we all retired to the living room, and my wife and I sat on a couch while TJ and her husband, Mark, sat on the floor. We were just talking and drinking some wine. Mark started to kiss his wife's neck, and so I started to make out with my wife. When I looked over a few minute later at TJ and Mark, they were both naked and kissing, with Mark fingering TJ's pussy. That was when I started to remove Judi's clothes, and, after she was naked, I took off my shirt. My wife and I continued to make out, and I was rubbing her breasts when I heard some moans and looked over to see Mark and TJ fucking.

I slid my hand down to my wife's pussy, and she was already soaking wet. As I was kissing my wife and fingering her, I noticed that TJ sat down on the couch next to Judi, and Judi just kept kissing me with her tongue down my throat.

After a minute I stopped kissing Judi, and turned her head toward TJ, and they immediately started to kiss. I just sat back, and Mark and I were watching. TJ started to caress my wife's body and to pinch her already hard nipples. She took her time exploring my wife's chest and stomach, and I noticed my wife was rubbing TJ's boobs and thighs. I also noticed how hard they were making out, and saw that my wife had started to separate her legs. TJ eventually started to slide her hand down and separate my wife's labia, and then entered her pussy with two of her fingers.

My wife immediately arched her back and moaned. TJ then slid my wife down and laid her diagonally on the couch with her legs separated and one leg on the floor while the other was on a cushion. Within a short time TJ moved between my wife's legs and started to eat her pussy and finger her cunt. My wife was going crazy with her head turning from side to side and moaning. I looked down, and Mark had gotten behind his wife and was fingering her pussy and looked at me, saying, "She is so wet!" I slid my hand over her butt and entered her with one finger, and I have to admit that not only was she wet, but she may have the slickest pussy I had ever felt. I continued to finger TJ's pussy, and Mark went up and sat next to my wife's head, and started to caress her boobs which made her even more aroused.

Soon TJ had four fingers in my wife, and was working them in and out of her pussy, and so I reached down with my fingers which moments ago had been in TJ's pussy and started to rub my wife's clit. She immediately start to buck and cum and cum. She finally caught her breath and I continued to rub her pussy, and TJ continued to work her fingers in and out of her cunt, and then almost immediately she yelled out, "Oh, I am going to cum again!"

My wife looked over at Mark sitting next to her, and stared at his hard cock only inches away from her face. Her face was flushed and her eyes were full of lust. Mark was still rubbing her tits and nipples, and for a minute, I thought my wife was going to reach out and grab Mark's cock and start to suck on it. Mark thought so as well, as he slid his pelvis forward, positioning his cock right next to her mouth. Judi started to raise her arm to take hold of his cock when another orgasm hit her hard and violently. She arched her back and screamed out as the intensity of her orgasm spread all over her. Judi reached down and pushed my fingers away from her clit and pushed TJ's fingers out of her pussy, as it was just too sensitive after the massive orgasm she had just experienced. Everything just started to subside at that point, and TJ walked over to the other couch, while Mark followed and spread his wife's legs and started to eat her.

I was so turned on that I could not wait any longer, and mounted my wife, driving my big cock into her, and she responded by grabbing my face and kissing me deeply, and then said to me, "Thank you for letting me experience what just happened." I drove my cock into her harder and, for some reason, decided to take my wife over to the couch that TJ and Mark were on, and had her lean over TJ's head as I took her from behind. TJ looked up and started to rub Judi's clit as I fucked her from behind. I then heard TJ start to cum from Mark eating her pussy, and that was all I could take, as I shot my load into my wife's pussy. Even before I had pulled out, I could feel my cum and my wife's juices starting to leak out from around my cock. My wife must have felt it as well, as she stood and said she needed to go to the bathroom.

I went back over to the original couch and watched Mark continue to caress TJ's pussy. TJ looked down at Mark and said, "I will finish you up later," and then laid back on the couch and looked at me, saying, "Wow, I am totally satisfied right now!"

I shook my head in agreement and said, "Me too!"

Mark got up and said he needed to go the bathroom as well, and left the room. TJ on one couch, and I on the other, just relaxed in post orgasmic bliss.

I was relaxing when I thought that my wife had been in the bathroom a long time, and then shortly after that I heard what I thought was a dull thud sound from the hall bathroom, and wondered what it was. Then I heard it again and again.

TJ and I both rose up on our elbows and looked down the hall, and for sure we both could hear the unmistakable sound of female moaning coming from the bathroom. I got up and walked down the hall, and looked into the bathroom, and my wife was sitting on the edge of the bathroom counter with her legs spread wide, and Mark was between her legs driving his cock into her wet hot pussy. The sight was so erotic, especially with what had just transpired! The thought then struck me that Mark had been the only one who had not gotten off yet among all of us. That accounted for why he was banging Judi with such intensity.

Looking at my wife's face, I could tell that she was not at all minding the attention. She had the face of one concentrating on an impending orgasm. I looked next to me, and saw that TJ was standing there rubbing her own clit while watching Mark fuck Judi. My cock had already come to full attention, and, from the sounds next to me, TJ was getting wet and preparing to get off again. TJ reached down and grabbed my cock and started to stroke it, and said to me, "That is so hot," to which I agreed. Within a few minutes one could tell by the look on Mark's face and his urgency that he was getting ready to cum. Then suddenly he stiffened and slammed hard into Judi's pussy and held his cock deep in her as he gave out a low moan. My wife then said, "Oh! I can feel you cumming in my pussy!"

Then she said, "I am going to cum again, don't pull out yet!" and with that Mark started to thrust again to help her have another orgasm. My wife started to say, "Oh my! Oh my!" and then looked at Mark and kissed him deeply.

That was when TJ spoke up and said, "Mark, you and Judi can have our bedroom for the night, we are going to the spare bedroom." She walked me down the hall and laid on the bed with her legs spread and said, "I have not had a cock in my pussy yet tonight, I need that hard cock in me NOW!"

I slid between her legs as my cock seemed to know where to go, and slipped completely into her pussy. I don't think we fucked very long before we both came and then we both fell asleep. Later that night I woke up and went to the bathroom to pee, and, when I came out I could hear sounds coming from the other bedroom. So I walked quietly to the door and I could hear the familiar sounds that my wife makes just before she has an orgasm. I could also hear the springs of the bed as Mark must have been pounding her pretty hard. There is something erotic listening to your wife getting fucked, maybe not as erotic as watching her being penetrated, but erotic enough that I continued to stand there at the door as I stroked my own cock. I went back to bed and in the morning TJ and I fucked again and took a shower together.

As Judi and I drove back to our room, I told her that I had heard them having sex in the middle of the night. She said that after they went to the bedroom they kissed and then fell asleep since they were both spent. Then in the middle of the night Mark woke her up and fucked her hard, and then again an hour or two later he fucked her again. I asked her if it was good and she said, "Hell, yes! I came twice the first time, and the second he lasted longer and I had three orgasms, but all close together."

We fucked like bunnies the next two days, both of us thinking about one of the most amazing evenings we had ever experienced.

Chapter Seven

Fit To Be Tied

Every day is a winding road we must all travel. What's around the next corner? Who will we see? What awaits us?

It was another one of those days, starting off with leisure time in my own bed, wondering what I'll encounter. I always imagine a lot of things, but reality always reminds me of what I will be doing when four o'clock rolls around.

But let's drive down imagination lane for a couple of miles and see what happens. What exciting detours might we explore? Maybe the bridge will be out. Maybe there will be a new cutoff to ride through. I'm beginning to see the bend in the road ahead. Shall we continue?

It was almost half past eleven when I arrived at adventure headquarters. The screen door had a note attached, and the main door was opened. I called out to see if anyone was in the house, but there was no answer. The note said they would be next door, should anyone be looking. I decided to venture in since the screen was unlocked.

I walked down the hall past the bathroom, and, as I got to the bedroom door and was walking past, I caught a glimpse of something. There on the massive bed was a large present. Covered in white and wrapped with black silk cord. I wasn't sure if the present was for me, but it was beautifully wrapped, and I found it hard just to look at it. I stepped through the doorway and took a closer look. Awesome!

The present was laying across the bed running the length of the white cotton sheets. She was wrapped in silk stockings from her feet to her waist. She was wearing a lacy white bra and her face was covered with a mask. Her hair was loosed and tossed about her face. She was bound at the ankles and knees, and her hands were tied to the bindings at the knees. She lay still and quiet as if in some great anticipation of an upcoming event.

I rolled her up on her knees and discovered that her ropes went around her waist and fit nicely in the crack of her perfect ass. Her creamy soles were exposed and her legs were as smooth as silk. She was gagged but made no sound as I touched her to move her. She lay there in complete submission, having no idea what was to become of her. My mind raced with ideas, and I narrowed it down to one hundred!

Her feet looked so inviting with her soles exposing the seams of her stockings. Those toes needed to be loosed from their captors, so I placed my key between her toes and made a small tear. I placed my fingers into the hole and tore an opening. I repeated the process on the other foot. I had to do it. They were so inviting. I sucked each one of her toes and she made her first sound. Something had come up in the process and was now wanting to make its presence known.

I was feeling a pull in my pants and someone wanted to play. I unzipped my pants and I'm sure I saw a cloud of steam escape. I pulled off my trousers and rolled her over on her back. I must have been there for hours tickling and kissing, and touching her all over. She responded in many ways, and I pushed her closer and closer to her limits of sanity. When I felt like I could take her no further, I motioned for her husband to come and finish her off. I untied his perfect gift and she exploded on my lap and went down on me hard. I think every ounce of energy in my body was spent and flowing down her cheeks.

I excused myself for the rest of the afternoon, as the present I had been given was now given to the rightful owner. Lord have mercy on him, for this was a gift, fit to be tied.

Chapter Eight

The Losing Game

Judi, Bill and I have had several threesomes together in the past. Bill and I both have gained too much weight, and Judi and I came up with a solution. I bet Bill one hundred dollars that I would lose more weight than him in a six month period. The deal was if we lost even a pound between weigh ins, we could have sex with Judi by ourselves, or the three of us together. The choice was made by the biggest loser at the time of the weigh in. We approached Bill with the idea and of course he was all in.

To celebrate, we weighed in and decided to have sex together to start the competition. I weighed less, so I got to choose the first position. Judi laid down and I began to eat her pussy, as Bill fed her his cock. He played with her breast as I ate her to her first of many orgasms. After she had cum the largest of all cums she got very weak and sensitive, and her clit became an inch long and that big around.

I told Bill to keep feeding her as I loosened her up for his horse cock. I slid into the bottom, and the velvety softness gripped me just like a pair of silk covered hands and began milking my cock. After a few minutes of ramming her as my balls swung against her ass, I told Bill it was time to switch ends. As he pushed his cock in slowly, I fed her my cock covered with her juices. He totally filled her up, and I could see her juices flowing out around his cock and turning everything white with her cream.

He began to plow her deeply, and she began moaning and cumming in waves as she swallowed my cock down her throat and breathed deeply through her nose. Bill couldn't last long with such a tight pussy, and began cumming in torrents as she came one last time with his cock buried to the balls inside her pussy.

After everyone began breathing again, I told her I still had not cum, and I told her I wanted a cream pie first, and then I would cum inside her also. I devoured her pussy from top to bottom and sucked out all the combined juices she had to offer as she came again and again while moaning. I told Bill to let her clean him up and he began getting hard again. When I finished all the sauce she had to offer, I raised her legs to my shoulders and began to fuck her hard and fast just the way she loves it.

She was sucking Bill to a wonderful stiffness again as I began cumming in her pussy. She felt me cumming in her pussy, and began cumming again with me. I told Bill it was his turn and he said he wanted to try a cream pie himself, and began munching and sucking her pussy from top to bottom as I watched, all the while playing with my cock.

We ended up swapping positions all evening as Judi made each of us hard again and again with her talented mouth and pussy. What a way to be the biggest loser. I think all three of us are going to love the next six months!

Chapter Nine

Déjà vu All Over Again

We'd barely left home and headed down the road when we arrived at our destination. The trip was hurled into high gear by our excitement for getting out of town and the myriad of words spoken in the conversation that seemed to never end. We were like school girls talking about everything that had ever happened to each other.

We poured ourselves out completely, and now we were bathing in our new friendship and loving it.

We both had needed to find a kindred spirit to cling to in those moments when the men in our lives went stupid and were no longer any fun. If it wasn't for sperm, I don't think women would need men at all, not with all the toys they have in the stores, if you know what I mean.

We unpacked our belongings and claimed the bed we wanted, and fought for first in the bathroom. We decided to go out and eat some good seafood and come back and give each other facials. It doesn't take long to find a good restaurant or a waitress who asked the right questions. "Are you sisters?" she asked. We laughed and said we were just friends down for a seminar. That was definitely understated, as we were about to find out.

We were tired when we got to the room, but remembered our promise. Servance was first for her facial. She half wrapped herself in a towel and laid across my bed. Her hair was pulled back behind her head and she had no make-up on. Her hands lay along her side and she pulled her knees up and had her toes hanging over the side of the bed. I thought someone would sure love to be here for this and make hay while the sun shone. She closed her eyes and trustingly lay still. I took the potion and began rubbing it softly on one cheek and then another. I traced around her lips and nose and then both eyes. She commented on my soft touch and I kept going.

When I was done she opened her eyes and said I was next. I grabbed my towel and pulled it tighter as I lay across my bed too.

She commented that I had no shame. I looked to see what she meant and realized my towel had quite the gap and I was definitely exposed. I quickly covered up and she commented on my clean shaven pussy. She said she had wanted to try that but was afraid it would itch too much. She was very matter of fact, but I was still blushing. She told me to lie back down and began applying the magic potion to my welcoming face. She said I hope I look this good, "When I'm your age." I thanked her and told her she was too kind. I thought about it as I closed my eyes, and pondered her words.

Servance's fingers seemed magical as she caressed my face. It was so comforting that I dozed off to sleep and was awakened by those magic hands massaging my feet with lotion. I could feel the strength in her hands as she applied pressure to each toe. She grasped my arch with a firm hand and reached deep beneath the surface to release pressure built up from weeks on my feet. "I see you abuse your feet like me. Yours are painted so pretty. Love the color. I wish my feet were prettier. Mine are so ugly. I'm almost embarrassed to go barefoot. Suzanne and Rainey have the cutest feet. Will and Mike must like feet. They keep theirs painted all the time. I'm not pressing too hard, am I?"

I couldn't believe she had picked up on Will's foot fetish that easy. If she only knew! "No, that feels better than my massage therapist. How long are we to keep this mud on?"

"It's about time. Do you want to shower first Passion?"

"I guess so. I'll save you some hot water. Can I borrow some shampoo? I forgot mine."

"I left it in the tub so it would be there when I needed it. Use whatever you need. I'll watch TV till you're through."

I hurried into the shower and cleaned myself. The water felt really good and the mud washed away easily. My face felt firm and I couldn't wait to look in the mirror and see the results. I wrapped my head into a towel and another around my warm moist body. I then rushed out and onto my bed, and yelled, "Your turn!"

Servance arose from her bed and walked into the bathroom. I heard all manner of sounds, and then silence.

I took my towels away and slid under the covers. My body had already warmed the sheets beneath me, and it was quite snuggly. When Servance walked back in she cut off the light and the TV, and climbed in her bed. She commented on her face feeling and looking better and thanked me. I thanked her too, especially for the foot rub. My feet still felt great. I wondered what she could do with a back and neck.

I had taken my medicine before going to bed, so I knew I was out of it. For some reason I woke up around six-thirty and was so surprised. I don't know how or when, but I was not alone when I awoke. I forgot I was on the road and turned looking for Jake, but found something quite different. The hand on my back was not rough at all but smooth, and had a French manicure.

"Good morning," she said, "Did you sleep well? I hope you don't mind but I couldn't sleep alone. I need to have someone in the bed with me and you are my only choice."

"No problem." I slept through it all and wondered what I had missed. I could tell my butt was exposed, and Servance confirmed it by stating she wished her ass looked that good. I thanked her for the compliment and she disappeared into the bathroom. When she emerged, she looked glorious. Her hair was inundated with soft curls, and she smelled heavenly. Her strappy high heels made her legs taut and long. Her black skirt and see through blouse were beautiful, they complemented her suede fifteen button vest. Her chest showed ample cleavage, and I even felt small looking at hers.

"You have my number and I'll call you when I get a break, or text you. What would you like for lunch? We break at twelve. Have a good day! Bye!"

She bent over and kissed me on the head, and I just sat there dazed and confused. I got up and dressed and looked at my new face. I fixed my hair and went to the car and headed out to my favorite destination, the mall.

Servance texted me to go to lunch at eleven forty-five, so I picked her up and we headed for Red Lobster. We had soup and salad and talked about everything but last night. I took her back to the hotel for her afternoon session, and she said she would be finished at five thirty. I drove away and headed for the little antique shop I saw earlier.

I came back to the hotel a little early and changed into a slinky dress, and, of course, I wore my usual underwear, none at all, given to me on the day I was born. There was a freedom to going bare, and it made me feel sexy all the time.

When Servance entered the room I was laying on the bed on my stomach reading a book and swinging my feet and legs in the air behind me.

"You better get ready, we're going to get some real food tonight."

"Give me a minute to freshen up and I'll be ready."

When she returned she had changed into a beautiful forest green dress flowing down to her feet, with a gorgeous belt. She had on peeping pumps with straps on the heels. Her left ankle was adorned with a silver anklet that was fashioned into sort of a charm bracelet, a very pretty piece. We leapt to the car and took off in a flash.

We found this cute cafe near the train station housed in a couple of old railroad cars. The menu had an array of food that only a master chef could have devised. The booths were decorated in splendid pieces, and the candle lighting was very becoming. Servance looked very pretty in the light, and her eyes seemed to twinkle. We ordered our wine and entrees, and it wasn't long before we were feeling it a little.

The food came and was glorious, we gorged ourselves, and then some. I for one was getting very tired. About that time I felt something up against my leg. At first I thought it was casual contact, and then I realized it was a bit more. "Are you going somewhere with this?" I asked.

She said, "Say when." I thought it a little funny so I kicked off my shoes and returned the favor. Servance said that felt pretty good. I told her it was the massage that made them softer. As Servance leaned back in the booth I felt my dress sliding up my calf and over my thigh. Now it was becoming a little warm. I could feel my juices flowing, and I was definitely getting in the mood.

Maybe I shouldn't have, but I said, "When!" Servance leaned forward and pressed her chest against the table, lifting it up.

We made it back to the hotel safely, and I took my shower first. My roommate was still attached to her wine goblet when I came out of the shower. She had pushed the door open just a little and was watching my reflection in the mirror on the wall in the hall. I dried off and wrapped my robe around me and went into the bedroom and laid on the bed. My hair was a little damp, and I told Servance I was pooped and ready for bed. She smiled and echoed my sentiments. I asked if she was sleeping with me again, and she said you never know. While she was in the shower, I took my sleep medicine and slipped off my robe and lay back on the bed. I must have really been tired for I don't even remember falling asleep.

Servance finished in the shower and put her hair up in a towel, and her robe on tight. She walked into the bedroom and couldn't believe what she saw. There I was, naked on the bed with my hands above my head, and my feet hanging off the bed. She said she called my name a couple of times, and then she took the sheet and mostly covered me up. She laid on her bed sipping her wine and just couldn't stop looking at my body forming quickly beneath the sheets. She could make out my tits and my hands and easily see my knees.

Unfortunately, she neglected to cover up most of my right leg and foot. I should have never told her she could rub my feet anytime. She took me literally. She called my name a couple of more times and then figured I was in a coma.

What happened next is pretty kinky. Servance rose from her bed and stepped over next to my bed. She carefully removed the sheet from my body and placed it on the chair. She opened up my bag to get some lotion and found my restraints. She grinned from ear to ear and a plan ensued. She figured out the restraints and began attaching them to my wrists and ankles. She attached the straps to the bed and the mattress frame. As I lay sleeping, she had tied me and pulled me to the four corners. I was still out of it when she slipped off her robe and climbed in next to me. She lay there, at first wondering what to do. She later confessed she couldn't help herself. She said my body looked like a goddess lying there, what a turn on she added. She found the lotion and started on my boobs and belly button.

It started as light rubbing and built to kisses and caresses. She expanded her borders and made it all the way down to my feet again. I was starting to come out of my deep sleep but wasn't aware of what was going on. And then it happened.

Servance began rubbing my tits between her fingers and must have had both of them. I was starting to wake and realized I couldn't move. I had trouble breathing and, as I gasped for a breath, I opened my eyes to see Servance straddled over me and kissing my neck. I turned my head to the right and saw my hand in a restraint. I pulled gently but it didn't move. I started to speak and I felt a finger slip into my mouth and the hush of her voice as she quieted me. By this time, I was quite surprised, but mostly aroused.

My chest began rising from the bed and my stomach contorted. Servance kept her finger in my mouth and I began to suck on it. She must have had some peppermint oil, for that finger tasted great. I could feel her breasts against me and the strength seemed to ooze from her body as she seemingly pressed against me everywhere. I even felt her anklet sliding across my legs. It felt cold and titillating. She slid down my belly and fixed herself right above my pussy. I tried to say when, but to no avail. She had me well down the turned on path, and I was ready to surrender.

The onslaught continued, as I felt her mouth descend on my clit, and her tongue assaulted me in every way imaginable. My pussy started gushing and she cried, "Oh, yeah! Oh, Yeah!" I was climaxing every thirty seconds and orgasms were turning me upside down on the inside.

After about an hour she stopped. I don't know why, I was thrilled beyond measure. I could hear her breathing as she pulled her finger from my mouth. She crawled off the top of me, and I could see the cum on her own leg. She had come down so hard on me she burst her own dam. I told her to untie me, and I would help her with that. She said no, she just wanted to look at my beautiful body and make herself cum one more time. I watched as she pleasured herself. Her muscles rippled beneath her beautiful skin and she looked so very, very, strong. Her nipples were hard and she was so cute with her hair all messed up.

I told her if she cut me loose I'd let her sleep with me the rest of the night. I knew I couldn't physically make her, and she knew it. I managed to cop a feel a couple of times through the rest of the night, but mostly just held her and told her I loved her. She ran her leg up the front of my body and I reached down and ran my hand up and down her leg and ankle, playing with her anklet. We both drifted off to sleep as I began to assess the events of the night. How was I going to process all of this?

My sleep was somehow not affected by this recess of love and sex. My pills put me back into the deep sleep my body needed. I awakened to bright lights and a rush of wind. When my eyes finally focused I realized I was in the car. I wondered how Servance had packed me and my stuff, and put me in the car.

Then she said, "You sure were sleeping soundly there. You must have had a whale of a dream. We'll be at the hotel in about twenty minutes. I brought some stuff to do some facials tonight. I'm going to have to find a way to wake you up so we can go out later."

About that time, I looked down and saw the anklet. I was flabbergasted. It was way too spooky! In a funny way I was really looking forward to the trip now. Déjà vu all over again.

Chapter Ten

Cool Summer Evening

It began as a normal evening. Friends had gathered for a night of fun and games, and everybody was winding down as was the sun. The shadows were growing longer and the candles danced with flames in their glass fixtures. The sky was a deep blue, almost purple. Everyone had found their favorite chair as the music subsided and I was on stage, entertaining my friends.

The guitar sounded rich and warm as I strummed the strings. The amplifier added a stirring chorus sound that was hauntingly beautiful. We all sang songs we knew and listened to the ones we didn't, but still I played on.

It became increasingly darker as each melody played. We all pulled in close to one another and I had my back to the window on the porch. In the circle around me sat the ones I loved and the ones who loved me.

Our guards were all laying on the floor, as one by one we revealed more of whom we were without any protection. The wine was starting to talk and have its effect on all of us. The darkness was complete in its settling around us and providing a shroud for the stars to back light the night.

I had not always been drawn to her, but that day was different. Her namesake had always kept me at a distance. There were things she did not like about herself and she rarely spoke of them. She had even convinced me the truth was in her statements. There were always burst of glory in her appearance. Sometimes it was her voluptuous hair. At times it was her beautiful eyes. Her clothes were always eye catching and impeccable, but never this before. And then it happened.

Without warning, and certainly without fanfare, she did the deed. While leaning back in her chair and sipping on her chalice of wine, she did the unexpected. She lifted her legs and placed her feet on the table in front of everyone, but especially me. A loaded gun could not have been more dangerous! I tried not to look, and became very uneasy. I almost stopped playing and then something strange happened. A dance began at her ankles and soon spread to her feet, and then her toes. The dance grew more and more, and moved right with the music. It was almost as if my fingers on the strings were manipulating every movement of her feet right before me. Everyone else seemed to fade into the background. I could still hear them singing and talking, but the spotlight was on these average feet which became superstars with one dance. They danced for hours with their weaving and rubbing and arching, seemingly for my delight. I knew no one, but I would enjoy this encounter, but would they quench the source to the point of her removing my dessert? However long, it wasn't long enough, and I watched as she withdrew her beautiful soles and slipped away to bed. The wine had overtaken her till tomorrow, and I was left empty and hollow with no chance to retrieve the hours.

I still have glimpses of her former charm. She pays some attention to those feet of hers. They have great potential, and have adorned many a shoe that has caught my fancy. But it has become the time of the year to put them all away and think of how to keep them warm for the fall and winter. I shall miss them until their triumphant return in the spring. Thank you for the last dance, I arise just thinking of your awesome display.

Chapter Eleven

Tracie's Deep Tissue Massage

"I can either bring a table, or we can do it on your bed or somewhere else." I was wearing sheer pants and no underwear. You could see my cock outlined in my pants but our massage began with professional and courteous conversation. I was wearing a form-fitting black t-shirt. You could see that my body was hard, smooth, and fit. I asked you what kind of physical ailments you were facing, what areas you would like me to focus on, and whether you had any injuries that I should be aware of.

We began with quiet relaxing music, perhaps some scents or incense if you prefered. I told you that you may undress to your level of comfort, get under the sheet face down, and that I would be back in a moment. While I was away you undressed entirely, pausing for a moment to decide whether you should remove your thong.

Your body was beautiful, smooth, and in need of a full massage. You decided to get completely naked, because that is the most relaxing state for you. You caught a glimpse of yourself in the nearby mirror and you were aroused by your feminine curves, your breasts, your waist, the shape of your pelvis, the firm roundness of your ass. I knocked and you told me to wait just a second. You climbed under the sheet, took a deep breath, and closed your eyes to relax.

We began with you lying face down. Your man could either be a part of the massage experience or we could begin in a very professional manner and have him walk in once we had really gotten down to things. It was your choice. You were under the sheet, warm, calm and relaxed. I rolled the sheet to uncover your shoulders. Warm lavender oil and cinnamon oil touched your bare skin. You felt my hands glide over you as I uncovered different parts of your body, focused on releasing tension in your muscles. I used different deep tissue methods to therapeutically release tension in your body. My hands were strong, warm, and pulsing with blood. You felt relaxed and electric at the same time. You began to feel wetness between your thighs, but told yourself that I was only the masseuse and not to get excited. I focused on your shoulders, your neck, your mid back, arms and hands. I slid the sheet all the way down to the curve of your ass, those beautiful dimples at the base of your strong back. The cotton sheet arousesed you as it passed over excited nerves.

At this point your entire upper body was uncovered. You had goose bumps. So did I, but we both tried to convince ourselves that this was a professional massage and nothing to get overly excited about. You were relaxed, feeling the tension in your body releasing in many ways, but the tension between us was building. You were aware that I could see the soft curve of your breasts, the sides just showing as you laid face down on the table. You were aware that you were gorgeous, that I saw your body as precious, that I admired your shape. Every man or woman who has seen you this way has. As I covered your back with the sheet again, the glow of oils pulsed through your upper body and your lower body longed for the same touch. Your loins were warmed, moist and pulsing.

As I passed by your side, my hard cock gently grazes your hand which rested still at your side. All at once you felt my throbbing, engorged eight inches thick with veins, muscle, blood and smooth skin. You imagined the head deep inside of you. You imagined the feeling of penetration, the gasp of air that we both released as I entered you, the arch of your back as you took all of me inside of you for the first time, touching spots that you didn't know were there. You imagined the feeling of my eight inches entering your lips, the drop of cum on your lips, your first taste of me. You imagined taking me all the way, me not being able to resist the back of your throat, my balls in your hands, pulling me closer, fingernails in my back, your thirst for more of this smooth hard cock. Your thirst for the way I seemed to keep getting harder in your warm mouth. You thirsted for the way my abs tensed under your touch when you spit on my cock and took it in both hands. You thirsted for the feeling of my strong arms pulling you closer as I lost control.

All of those thoughts occurred in a single moment, a single brush of the length of my cock, a single rush of blood to your clit, your inner thighs, a single rush of wetness that emerged from the smooth lips of your pussy. You didn't know it, but I was imagining many of the same things, wondering about the warmth of your lips, the taste of your wet labia, the ridges of your wet pussy. I was wondering whether you could take all of me into your mouth, wondering whether you would choke a bit on my cock and push me away, covered in spit, your eyes watering, your body craving more. You wondered how long it would take you to beg me to fill your pussy with my throbbing cock, wondering how long I would tease you until I let you have it.

But that single moment passed. I was still clothed. You were wetter than before, your clit was swollen, the air was humid. My heart was racing. My hands were firm on your back. My cock was still hard. My hands were still covered in oil. The sexual tension was palpable, the air was to saturated with our lust, our respect for each other's bodies, our desires, that we both had to exhale so that we were not consumed by the oxygen that surrounded us.

I tried to tell myself that this was inappropriate. I was your masseuse. I was here to heal your body. To ease your tensions. I continued to touch you, savoring your skin, pressing deeper into your muscles, listening for your light muffled moans, the sound of your voice as you bit your lip, denying your desire to turn over on the table and take me right there.

I massaged your head, your scalp, your earlobes, your temples. You could feel the electricity of my cock close to your lips. You bit your lip harder, all that you could do not to lift your body from the sheets and take me in your mouth. Your nipples were hard, even against the moist cotton that was below you. Just as your willed yourself to reach for me, I moved around the table again, this time I did not graze your hand, but you could feel the heat coming from my body against your palm anyway.

I rolled the sheet to your knee and slowly rubbed oil on your calves, your feet, your knees, and the soft skin behind your knees. I began to massage your feet, focusing on tension-relieving pressure points, stretching your toes, rubbing them slowly. I worked my way up your calves, pressing with the heel of my hand, deep. Your fire was still burning. You pelvic curve was still swollen with desire, your lips still longing. I started rolling the sheet slowly up to reveal your thighs, smooth, toned and fit. You felt my cock against your hand again as I worked my way up the side of your body. You did not pull away. You pressed so slightly against it, feeling it grow.

I massaged your thighs, aroused from the simple touch of the back of your hand. Your thighs were warm. The muscles were tight. I worked slowly closer and closer to your inner thigh, pausing to apply oil, you were growing wetter and I could feel it. I worked my hands closer and closer to the muscle of your groin, careful not to get too close to your pussy, more out of respect for our professional relationship. As I rolled the sheet to expose your hips I was surprised to find that you were wearing no underwear at all. Your bare pussy was exposed to me, and the emerging wetness glistened on the surface of your swollen lips. Deep breaths kept my hands moving, stroking your thighs with strength and precision. I held your pelvis and pressed firmly on your hips to readjust. It's rare that clients are fully naked and I wasn't sure if I should stop or keep going.

I massaged your inner thighs and my fingertips began to feel the wetness that had accumulated over almost thirty minutes of agonizing restraint. I hesitated and began to cover your body with the sheet, but I was arrested when I heard you say, "Yes."

"Excuse me, ma'am?"

You moved your body down the table closer to me so that my hand collided with the dripping lips of your pussy. It was a subtle move and I was nervous, but I didn't want to stop. You said it again, "Yes."

I took the cue, but I took it slowly. I began to massage your inner thighs and lightly apply the oil to your pussy and the introductory curve of your lower back. You felt my warm fingertips graze your clit. Neither of us spoke. I began to massage your groin. It was smooth and delicate, so I was delicate with my touch. Slowly my hands moved onto the lips of your pussy, and I massaged you with a firm touch. Oil, your wetness, my sweat, the smell of our pheromones, I was massaging your pussy, rubbing your clit with both hands. Your back arched. You reached for my cock. Your hand found my ass and pulled me against your side. My cock was fully against your ribs. You could feel the head of it. Your imagination then let go and reality took hold.

You told me, "More!" and I slowly inserted one finger while I massaged your ass, wondering how far this would go. You pulled me closer against you. I put another finger inside and reached for your g-spot. You were still face down and I longed to massage your breasts.

"Should we stop? What about your husband?"

You didn't say anything. You just pulled me closer, your hand gripped my ass. Suddenly you grabbed my pants by the waistband, leading me around to the head of the table. I followed your lead and began massaging your lower back, my two fingers still in your pussy, lightly rubbing against your asshole. But you had been thirsting for this whole cock. You could feel my length, my girth. You wondered if you could take all of it.

You pulled the waist of my pants down and pulled yourself up slightly onto your knees. As your body created a 'V' on the table, I could see your beautiful breasts, curves articulated by gravity, nipples hard. Slowly, and with your eyes on me for the first time, you took me in your mouth. I was shaved, smooth, hard, and just as large as you had hoped. You sighed as you took my deep, and I continued to massage your back. I reached for your pussy but I was just out of reach, gripping your ass and lower back.

Your hands took mine as my cock reached the back of your throat. You guided them to your beautiful breasts, which felt perfect in my hands. Then you took your hands and held my lower back, while I massaged your arched back. You pulled my closer, deeper, you want more of me. You pull me closer and turned over, keeping my cock in your mouth as you rotated, sharing your gorgeous stomach and breasts with me. From here I could touch you better and see you better. You felt me tense up, my ass firm in your hands, my abs hard against your touch, the base of my cock smooth and sweet tasting. You leaned your head back to take me deeper as I put two fingers inside of you again. My muscular arms were warm against your skin and hard against your breasts. My forearms rested against your abdomen, warm and solid.

My cock was warm, throbbing, hard against your lips, against the back of your throat. I was gentle, but I filled your mouth, and you wanted me more while I was still massaging your abdomen and fingering you. My fingers are large and strong and they filled you, but not quite the way you wanted to be filled. You moaned as I pulled out, wondering whether this is forbidden, but you grabbed my balls and pulled them into your mouth, sucking hard, and I moaned as you tongued them with my cock, hard and wet from your spit, filling your hands. I realized that I didn't even want to escape this moment, and that I really wanted to taste your pussy that I had been imagining the entire time I had touched you. I massaged your breasts as you took me back in your mouth, tilting your head back again.

Suddenly you felt my cock shift angles in your mouth and opened your eyes to see that I had climbed on top of the table and was kneeling over you, my eager mouth reaching for your pussy. Slowly I hovered as you took me deep. But it was too deep, as my breath grazes your clitoris and you took me out of your mouth, gasping for air, feeling the saliva drip from my cock. You felt my breath, warm, slow, heavy. You felt the oil still lingering on your inner thighs as I rubbed you. You gripped my cock hard with one hand as you pressed my face between your legs with the other.

You felt my humid kiss on your pussy. It tasted sweet and ready, ripe and knowing. Slowly I worked my tongue around your clitoris, breathing heavily, tasting your wetness. You took my cock back in your mouth, wet, hard, eager. We didn't realize how loud our breathing was, how heavy our muffled moans were, mouths occupied but never satisfied. You held my ass and pulled me deep into your mouth with one hand and buried my head between your legs with the other. You pulled my cock out of your mouth, letting it rest hard and wet against your neck so that you could concentrate on the feelings pulsing through your entire abdomen.

I inserted one finger, then two, then three, deep, while I slowly massaged your clitoris with a hard flat strong tongue, building speed, building force. I curved my fingers toward your stomach, finding your g-spot, massaging your lower abdomen with my other hand. You felt it building, slowly, both hands pressed my head down hard into your humid loins. I loved the way you tasted, the wetness filled my mouth, and I wondered if you would enjoy a lubricated finger in your ass, wondered if I should wait for your signal or slide you to the edge of the table and enter you with my cock, wondering if I should give you a heavy warm load of cum in your mouth, on your breasts, on the lips of your pussy, before I entered you, or if I should have saved it all for one climax. I decided to wait. You deserved everything I had, though it was hard to control myself.

You reached for my cock with your mouth again, but I pulled away, holding back my cum. You were pleasuring me so intensely that I had to tense my abdomen to keep from cumming all over your face right there and then. I began to pleasure your clit faster and faster, your back arched, you were speechless. Your body was lifted by a warm effervescence. Your legs shook as I pressed hard against your clit, my tongue then moving rapidly and rhythmically. Suddenly you grabbed my head and buried my face in your pussy, my fingers deep. You were cumming, hard, long, waves of full-body pleasure, your breath dangerously fast paced. You gyrated your hips, pulling my face hard against your pelvis, grinding against me. I felt a new wetness emerge, sweet, hot, flowing with the rush of your breath. I breathed in, only growing harder from your ecstasy.

I gave you a moment, wanting you to enjoy the phosphorescent glow of your orgasm while I savored the taste of your wetness on my lips. I massaged your abdomen. Breathing deeply with you, I looked into your eyes. Just then I spun you around to the edge of the massage table, and slid my throbbing cock deep inside of you, your lips closed gracefully around me. We both gasped, deep and exhaling, an ecstatic disequilibrium overwhelmed our bodies. We have craved and you could not have me deep enough, you craved, hungered, the tasted of my cock still in your mouth. I kissed you long and deep with a heavy tongue, the same tongue that pleasured your clit. You tasted your own cum on my lips and tensed around my cock.

I took you there, on your back, wrapped the sheet around your lower back and levered our bodies against each other. The slap of my balls against your ass made you long for things you had never done before. The scent of our sweat was deep in your nostrils, the glow of your first orgasm of the night was still pulsing through you with every thrust. I went slowly, moved my hips, held your legs above your head, teased you with the tip until you forced me back inside, deep, filling. I pulled out and rubbed the head of my cock against your clit. Slowly at first, then faster as your breath built, leading you to the edge of orgasm but plunging deep inside of you just as you were about to cum, teasing your nipples with my tongue.

Suddenly I thrust myself inside of you and you felt a weightlessness, a new depth. I lifted you off of the table and suspended you, my hands gripping your ass from both sides. I fucked you like this, fast, hard, and deep. I slowed down, thrusting deeply, deliberately, with a hard staccato, and pulled all the way out and entered your lips over and over, lingering just above your clit. Suddenly I raised you to my face. I wanted to taste you again, could not wait to taste you again. I turned you so that you could take my cock back in your mouth while I tasted your sweet pussy.

But my desire to fuck you from behind overwhelmed every other sensation, and I turned you back to the ground, pressing you against the massage table, my cock hard between the cheeks of your ass. I slowly rubbed against you, lubricated by your wetness, your saliva on my cock, and the oil that served as a reminder of your first thoughts of penetration. Just as the velocity of our grinding began to peak I bent you over the table, my hands firm against your hips, and I spread your ass cheeks to enter your tight pussy from behind.

From here I was deeper than you've felt me before, the head of my cock soft against your vaginal canal, everything else hard and pulsating. I held your breasts gently and slowly searched for the angle to hit your g-spot. "Tell me where you like it best." You told me and I continue to build there. I pulled your hair lightly, "Do you like that?" My breath was hot against your ear. I massaged your back heavily, bringing more blood to your pussy, building capacity, wetness, desire. You felt my abs hard against your ass, my hands strong against your back. I reached for your breasts again to pinch your nipples. Maybe you never felt this before, but it sent waves of pleasure through your entire body. I was inside of you, your wetness dripped down your inner thighs, onto the table. I was moving faster and faster, you gasped for it harder and harder. I slowed to tease you, to delay the wave of orgasm that I knew would take you some place you've never had been before. Just as I was speeding up again we heard the sound of a closing door.

From there it really depended on what role your husband wanted to play. Either he had been watching the entire time, or he had been in another room. He entered the scene, excited to see you, home from work early, and eager to make love. He was dressed in his work clothes and felt relaxed.

We slowed, but couldn't stop, our senses were blurred by the lust that pulsed through our veins. Your husband entered through door that faced us, your face was pressed against the table, my eyes on the curve of your back. He stopped for a moment, "What the fuck?" frozen.

I slowed my thrusting to stop. We were all speechless, silent, and he felt the air thick with lust. "I thought you were getting a massage?"

I began to pull out, but you reached behind and pulled me deeper. "I am!" I was not sure what to expect and considered running, but your pussy was so tight, so warm, so wet, and I wanted you more than ever. You noticed that your husband's cock had grown hard in the time that he had been in there. To break the silence you motioned him over. You grabbed his cock through his pants and began to stroke it. I was still deep inside of you, but unsure of what would happen next. I suppressed my desire to continue fucking you. As you unzipped your husband's pants and took him in your mouth, you began to rock against me, feeling my abs against your ass again, and my balls slapping against your thighs. You bounced against me, alternating between the depth of my cock in your pussy and the depth of his in your throat. All at once you were consumed by an overwhelming feeling of lust, greed for these two cocks that were penetrating you, filling you, you took us both deeper and deeper, all of our breathing collided in the dense air. His moaning was louder, my grunts staccato behind you, your moans long unmediated.

You instructed both of us that you were close. "I want both of your cum," you said, stroking his cock as your lungs reached for air. His hands were behind your head, on your breasts, down your back. My hands gripped your ass, maybe insert a finger if you liked. You had never been completely filled before, and it put you over the edge. Warmth pooled in your abdomen, then spilled to your thighs, emanating from your heart to the tips of your fingers and toes, warm light filled your body.

You pulled his cock all the way inside of your mouth and mine all the way inside of your pussy, all the way to the base for the first time.

As his cum began to spurt from the tip of his engorged cock, your orgasm peaked once, and, as it began to roll downwards, you felt the warm explosion of my cum in the depths of your abdomen and noticed that my hand had reached under your body to your clit, which I was stroking knowingly. Just as you felt yourself full with my hot cum and your clitoris rippling with warm sensations, your orgasm peaked again, your legs convulsing and a new wetness emerging from your pussy all over the base of my cock as I began to thrust again. He held your head deep, your lips wet and wanting around the base of his cock. You were filled with both of our cocks, with both of our cum. You could feel my cum beginning to drip from the lips of your pussy, slowly rolling down your thighs.

You pushed him away to gasp for air, satisfied, overwhelmed, perhaps only more desirous than before. You rose to stand and slowly let the full mouth of pearly cum flow down your chin and over the roundness of your breasts. It was hot against your skin, as was mine against your thighs. It almost reached your calves as the ecstatic glow softened and a deep warmth overwhelmed your body. My cock, still hard, slowly slid from your engorged lips. You rested against the massage table, your nipples sensitive to the slightest contact. Covered in cum, your body was warm, your palms were glowing, your body was still.

From here the question became, exactly how insatiable were you? There were two men with hard cocks ready to fuck you again. Your body was more ready than ever. Did you instruct me to leave so that you could fuck your husband properly? Did you instruct me to watch you fuck your husband? Did you instruct us to take turns fucking you? After all of this, if you were still desirous, what could possibly satisfy you?

Chapter Twelve

Passion

As I approached the door at the end of the hall, I noticed a strange light emanating from a portrait on the wall. The beautifully crafted gold frame seemed strangely dim compared to the image on the canvas. As I stopped to study the subject on the canvas I was overwhelmed by dizziness, and I seemed to lose consciousness.

I awoke to find myself alone and standing at what seemed to be foothills. In fact they were feet appearing to be twenty feet tall. I decided to work my way around them and see where I really was. And, as I stepped around the side, I saw a chiseled ankle and a long leg stretching forever. I reached over and felt the smooth surface. It was then that I noticed the ropes surrounding the legs and leading off to the west. I decided to go back the other way and found there was another foot and leg tied with the same ropes.

I needed a better view so I began to climb up the side of the closest foot. As I reached the summit I could see I was standing on top of what seemed to be a giant sculpture. I was standing on one of two beautifully painted feet. The toes were smooth and round and perfect. I could see the ropes reaching to the corner of the canvas and they were drawn tight.

I had to see more, so I made my way up the legs over the next hour and soon arrived at a beautiful garden. It seemed warm there and I noticed a crevice that had developed between the two legs. I decided to explore. As I descended into the crevice the temperature was definitely rising. I reached over to the walls on either side of me and I felt something move. My first inclination was to climb back up, but as I did I kept sliding back down. The surface was slippery and the more I climbed, the wetter it got until my clothes were completely soaked. I finally managed to climb back up to the flat surface. It was getting darker so I moved north, almost falling into a shallow hole someone had left uncovered.

I could now see the mountains that were formerly in the distance, were not mountains at all but beautiful, shapely, breasts. I leaned up against the face of one of them and the ground moved yet again. I made my way around them over the next thirty minutes or so and then way up north to an outstretched arm. It was sleek and taunt as I carefully walked past the elbows. I wasn't sure, but I believed I saw ropes leading off from the wrist towards the edge of the canvas. I thought the hands were discolored, until I realized they were painted.

The fingers were extended and seemed to be reaching for something. I decided to go back towards the breast and see what else I could see.

As I reached the neck I could see a curtain of some kind had been placed across the face of the statue. I could hear the wind blowing as I drew closer. It seemed to be speaking somehow. I made my way up to the other arm and found the same bound hand on that side reaching for freedom. The ropes were once again stretched towards the edge of the canvas. I then worked my way up to the top of the head so I could see all around.

What a sight! To the east and the west I could see outstretched arms reaching as far as the horizon. To the south lay the long legs with the chiseled ankles and the pretty toes. I felt my cock starting to enlarge. It was definitely a turn on to see this sculpture of a woman. It was so life like. I felt my penis growing out of my pants as I began to be dizzy once again.

I awakened near the crevice again, but this time it was smaller, or was I bigger? It wasn't a crevice at all, but a vagina. I had the urge to put my swelling penis right there. By this time I was getting thirsty, so I decided to drink from this well instead. What a decision that turned out to be! As I applied my tongue, a groaning could be heard audibly. I placed my tongue against it again, and this time I twirled it multiple times. An immediate surge took place and I realized I was exacting some kind of response from the statue. She seemed to be coming to life right in front of me. She surged against the ropes that bound her. Her chest rose and fell time and again and her bosoms tossed back and forth. The beauty of the rise and fall was very compelling. I reached up with my hands and steadied them by pinching her tits. That might have been a mistake for she gushed around her vagina and nearly drowned me. I took a deep breath and plunged my tongue deep into her and she responded my pinning my head between her thighs. I pressed my hands into her breasts and the undulation continued as her chest rose high above my head. If not for the ropes that bound her, I shudder to think what could have happened.

By now I had grown back to full size and realized I was as long as she was. I could feel her feet touching mine, and my hands reached hers, and she clung to my fingers with great force. I felt a huge presence beneath me and knew my penis had reached its peak size. I wedged myself between her hips and thrust myself deep into her vagina over and over, and over again. The ropes held and I exploded after nearly thirty minutes of pounding Passion.

Her breathing was heavy as I rolled to the side. She was spent, as her labored breathing subsided to shorter pants. I was still wet from her explosion in my face. The air around smelled of love-making and raw sex. I was back to normal as much as I could be, and it was time to reveal the eyes behind the veil. I reached over and gently pulled the silk from her eyes as tears streamed from the corners. She still didn't speak, but her eyes spoke volumes.

It was time to remove the restraints. I took my pocket knife from my shirt pocket and began cutting away the ropes, first the feet and then the hands. When I released those hands I released more than I could imagine. Passion flipped me over like a pancake and ripped my clothes from my body, leaving me naked and exposed. My penis had been half limp, but now rose to full strength as Passion pinned my legs to the canvas and thrust my penis into her moist warm mouth. Her right hand slid up under and grabbed me by the balls and tugged away. I felt my mind blacking out from the sheer ecstasy of her touch, and her tongue sucking and licking and blowing softly on my cock. I could feel the rush as my erection was so hard it hurt and the orgasm was coming like an avalanche. In a second I exploded like a can of whipped cream in the microwave, and there was Passion, licking it up everywhere. The cum dripped from her lips as her hands choked my penis into continued submission. I'm pretty sure I passed out at that point.

When my eyes opened I was standing in front of the canvas once again. The dim light still had its eerie presence and the picture still looked the same. I now knew what the artist was trying to show me in the drawing. Passion was not just a person, she was a lifestyle, a way to enjoy life's greatest pleasure. She had placed me on the canvas to experience all I had ever wanted to see and more. Passion had exceeded my imagination.

As I turned to leave, I spotted a woman at the other end of the gallery. She wore a painted dress, sexy shoes, and a smile that made me think I knew her. As I walked by I figured out who she was. Without a doubt she was the artist who had painted Passion on the canvas. I know knew, for she was the Passion I had felt. She had taken me to a place I may never yet see again. I am so glad I have my memories. I can't wait to come back to the gallery for some more art appreciation.

Chapter Thirteen

Passion's Power

Passion recently passed a milestone on her life. It wasn't a stone or really a mile away, but that's what they call them. She had a big celebration surrounded by all who loved her and wanted to be closest to her on that special day. She was showered with love and affection and many gifts, but still felt lacking. She curled up with a beer or two, and some wine and champagne. Later she would feel it without feeling any pain.

She spent the night waltzing back and forth between the venues, and finally stopped to watch the game a minute or two. Slowly she succumbed to the alcohol and laid back further and further until she was prone on the couch with her feet dangling off the end.

In some worlds that's agitating. In other worlds it goes unnoticed. In my world it turned into a show and a challenge. I couldn't take my eyes off the scene in front of me, as dangle after dangle drew my eyes like a magnet. I felt myself getting stiff with every second and wondered if anyone else knew what was going on. I wondered if even Passion could tell. The dance continued, so I placed a blanket across my lap as if I was cold.

That didn't draw any attention, so I slipped my hand down and felt just how hard my cock was. It was a struggle, but I slipped it down my pants leg and freed it under the blanket. I thought how good it would feel to have a foot job with these lovely feet in front of me. I took another blanket and covered Passion's feet and legs, and immediately they shot over to my lap and began searching for the prize. They inched their way slowly up and down my leg, causing me to grow stiffer. I reached under the cover and found the soles of her feet and then her toes, so alive and groping at everything. It was all I could do to hold in my excitement. As a precaution I added another blanket to disguise the mischief below.

In the deep confines of all this camouflage, two entities were searching for their counterpart. The one looking to attack, and the other waiting to be ambushed. The intensity picked up again. As Passion slid further down the couch her legs extended to her final destination. Her feet swept back and forth beneath the shorts and underwear to my nut sack, and lifted them as if spiking a football and letting them fall back under her toes. Over and over she thrashed, and then pulled back to my cock and began trampling it under foot, but then soothingly brushing up and down to an extreme point. I reached for her feet again and began rubbing softly over every inch to paint a mental picture in my head of the sneak attack I was experiencing. I was afraid I would cum right there and make a mess under the cover and all over me and her feet.

The attack was beginning to subside as the alcohol had done its dirty work, rendering Passion into a deep sleep and my thrill to a swift end. I wondered how it would be if we were alone. I wondered if I would have my way with her, or just strip her naked and take a million mental pictures of her beautiful sleeping body. Or could I awaken her by gently licking her pussy and manipulating her clit to wake her to a moment of climax and gushing body fluids.

When she awakened, Passion arose and left the building as one ship passes another. She touched the back of my neck as she passed, and a smile glimmered from her puckered lips as I watched her white ankles dance out the door. I sat there watching the game and waited for my monster to return to his cave. He would have to be satisfied on another adventure into Passion's world. That night was finished like a bowl of corn flakes that had been milked into oblivion.

Chapter Fourteen

Passion's Lament

You've heard about the cougar, How she drives this boy insane.

But I tell you now quite truly that she's just a pretty thing. But if you want the best of all the best things ever made, then you've got to have some Passion.

Only one to make the grade,

Passion takes the best of you and turns it up a notch.

It doesn't matter who you're with or what you think is hot, you've got to have some Passion or it isn't feeling good. You've got to have some Passion

Cause she loves you like she should

You'll find you're never satisfied cause no one else is great. When you're tired of having hamburger, Passion is your steak. Passion's all around me, she could take me in my car

Driving in a van she could take me pretty far

Or right across the table with her feet up in my lap. Or laying right beside me on the couch taking a nap. She can do more with her finger

Than another with both hands.

When she puts her tongue around me, I'm in the promised land

Passion's got her twins she can cover my whole face. Her legs are tight and pretty from the floor up to her ass.

Her hands upon my shifter just a changing all my gears. Or her body pressed against me just erasing all my fears.

Her shoulders soft and lovely flowing down her agile back. And she'd have a perfect bottom if it didn't have a crack.

Chapter Fifteen

Samantha's Amazing Massage

I'm a massage therapist, a good one. Being married, a senior citizen of 65, I am often amazed at the number of younger women who have gone out with me because of my age. I would guess that at least partly due to me asking them. I have always thought, if you don't ask, don't blame it on the girl if you have to sleep alone. I live in a nice little two bedroom home, comfortably far from my neighbors to enjoy a good deal of privacy. This privacy is especially welcome since on warm summer evenings I love to languish, sans clothes, in the hot tub with a beautiful lady. This is usually followed by her receiving my best erotic massage on a table I set up on the deck surrounding the hot tub.

Actually there are several versions of my massage, but occasionally I pull out all the stops and combine everything I know into one mind-blowing, multi-orgasmic massage for the lady. I have never had any complaints.

Several years ago I received a call from a lady I had known since she was in high school. Samantha was only 25, and younger than most of the women I had dated, so we had never been out. I realized I hadn't seen her in several years. As we caught up on the phone, I learned she had been away to college most of the time, and was now free to pursue her interests in the world of entertainment.

Samantha wanted to be an actress. She also wanted to book an appointment for Saturday. I explained that maintenance in my office building was using this weekend to hammer and bang things and repaint all the offices. "I do have a home office if you would be comfortable coming there," I offered.

"Sure, I'm okay with that. I have been a little depressed lately and I thought a nice relaxing massage would help me get over the blues. I'll explain the details when I see you Saturday."

I assured her I would do my best to ease her suffering. I also told her to be sure she wasn't in a hurry when she came. Since she had never had a massage with me before I didn't know precisely how long it would take. She said she did have a date later in the evening, so her time would be somewhat limited. We agreed on four o'clock in the afternoon.

On Saturday, after my one o'clock appointment left I checked my iPhone and there was a voice mail from Samantha. She was running a little late, but told me not to worry about needing to rush. She had canceled her date because the massage was more important to her, and her entire evening was free. So I wasn't surprised when Samantha didn't arrive until nearly five o'clock. When I opened the door I must have looked pretty ridiculous, because I did a double-take and just stared at her for several seconds longer than was decently expected. She began to fidget and asked, "May I come in, or is the massage going to take place here on your front step?"

I was able to recover quickly and said, "Sure! Come in. It is really good to see you after so long."

"I assume you really mean that," she said with a twinkle in her eye. "You sure took your time looking me over. Did you like what you saw?"

"Yes, I sure did," I responded. "I was just surprised by how beautiful you have become. I was expecting the skinny little girl I remember from your high school years. If you still aren't in a hurry, we could talk a while and catch up."

Samantha settled on one end of the couch and tucked her legs up under her. She was wearing loose, fire-engine red shorts and a very thin, loose, white tank top. Both were revealing enough that it wasn't long before I was pretty sure she wasn't wearing any underwear. Her body appeared to be lean and well-toned. It was obvious she worked out regularly. Also, her tank top revealed that, although she only had medium sized breasts, probably a B cup, she had huge nipples, and they appeared to be trying to poke through the material of her tank top, or maybe that was just wishful thinking on my part.

I confirmed iced tea was okay with her and went into the kitchen to get us both a tall glass. When I returned Samantha had shed her sandals and was thumbing through a massage magazine that was laying on the coffee table. I set her iced tea on a coaster on the table at her end of the couch, and went to the other end facing her with my own drink in hand. We chatted for some time, about her and her parents, my old girl friends, and many other things. It was a surprisingly comfortable conversation for both of us.

Finally I got around to business. After all, she was a client here for a massage. "So, have you ever had a full body massage from a professional massage therapist?" I asked.

She answered, "No, but I have had some pretty extensive massages by boyfriends and a few girlfriends. Does that count?" She looked at me with hooded eyes that nearly caused me to lose faith in my ability to be a professional.

But again I recovered. She had a way of catching me off guard that was a little embarrassing and totally cute. I loved it. Then Samantha asked me a question that really surprised me. She said, "I've been told that a really good erotic massage can help release emotional trauma. Is that true?"

I explained, "Deep, emotional trauma is an emotional energy pattern that sometimes gets 'stuck' in body tissues. When that happens, an erotic massage often helps, especially if the therapist knows what he is doing and what type of trauma he is dealing with. For instance," I went on, "trauma based on anger is often held in tissues near the liver, while trauma based in love or hate may be near the heart. Everyone is different. And there are no guarantees. I have had clients who released big and some who never released at any level." I stopped talking and waited to hear her response.

It was slow in coming. She lowered her head and eyes and began to talk. "About a year and a half back I had a boyfriend. He got really drunk one night and beat me up. Then he ripped off my clothes and raped me. All he would have had to do was ask, and I was his. I really liked him, but the alcohol changed him. I came out the other side of this event without a boyfriend and I haven't had an orgasm since. In fact, I even quit dating all together. And I haven't had any desire to masturbate either. All of these are out of character for me. I somehow sense this isn't healthy, so I decided to do something about it. After seeing several quacks and spending a lot of money, I still don't feel any better. Is this something you can help me with?" she pleaded.

I had to be honest, "I don't know. I've had some good results in the past, but also I've had some failures. The only way to know is to try it and see."

I decided it was time to start the massage, and I led Samantha back to the massage room. I explained she could undress to whatever level she was comfortable with, and get under the top sheet face down with her head in the cradle. Before I left her alone to carry out my instructions, I lit several candles and put some Eucalyptus oil on the headrest cover to aid in her breathing while she was prone. I flipped on the CD player that was preloaded with several massage music CDs. I pointed out the bathroom door and left to use the other bathroom to wash up before I started.

When returned I saw that Samantha had followed my directions perfectly. She was even centered on the table. I moved to the head of the table and placed my hands on her back with the palms resting over the hollow between her shoulder blades and her spine, near to her neck. I then allowed energy to flow from my hands to her body. I held this position for nearly four minutes until she let out a huge sigh and seemed to sink into the table more comfortably. Then I moved to the side and placed my right hand just below her sacrum and my left at the nape of her neck. I again let the energy flow, this time until I could feel the pulsing flow between my two hands. Again, as the energy started to pulse, Samantha let out a sigh, this one much more subtle than the first. "I'm going to pull the sheet down now," I told her.

She made a sound that sounded like, "umph, huh," which I took to mean okay, so I pulled the sheet down to her buttocks, just below the cutest dimples in her backside. I positioned her arms on either side with a slight bend in the elbows. I have an extra wide massage table that lets clients lie comfortably without worrying about their hands and arms falling off. My first look told me what a rare gem I had on the table. Samantha's skin was a flawless field of tanned human flesh with no indication of tan lines. It was smooth and well-toned. There were no blemishes or body markings of any kind. She was radiant and stunning. I can't imagine how someone, not even a drunk, could attack such a beautiful creature as this woman on my table. I vowed to myself at that point to do absolutely everything I could to get her back to her usual bubbly self.

I asked her if it was alright to remove the sheet completely, telling her that if she felt the need or if she got chilly that I would put it back instantly. She readily agreed, so I pulled the sheet away and continued on the journey with this beautiful, naked goddess.

I selected a potent jasmine massage cream because it was so feminine. I instructed Samantha to simply receive everything that followed. She was not to help, not even to reposition her body, unless I asked her to. I began the massage at her shoulders, using a small amount of cream and spreading it over a large area. This particular cream had a better texture than most, and it was easier to massage deeper without gliding over the surface. I wanted the effects of this massage to penetrate to the deepest muscles. Sometimes a much more slippery oil made that difficult to do.

I then moved slowly, gradually increasing the length of my strokes until I was moving from the top of her shoulders to her beautiful butt. The slow movement allowed the energy in my hands to flow into Samantha's skin and body. When energy flows into a muscle it tends to relax until you decide to use it. I wanted her muscles to be totally relaxed as soon as possible. After about ten minutes of long strokes from shoulder to buttocks, I moved to one side and trailed a hand on the body over her left butt cheek and down to her left foot. I used both hands to lift her left leg and move it toward the side of the table so her legs were flat on the table with her foot over the edge, toes pointing to the floor. I then lifted her left foot and spent at least a minute and a half or more on each of the major acupressure points on the bottom of her foot. I massaged each point with strong fingertips, pressing harder after the first minute so the pressure was going in deep. I then returned her foot back to the table with the toes hanging over the edge. I pressed and held the Achilles tendon to each side until I felt the connected muscles release. I then moved to the outside of her leg and began slow cross-fiber strokes with my entire hand. I used light pressure the first pass. My movements took me from her ankle to the knee and back. The next pass I pressed a little harder, but continued to move very slowly using the soft outer edge of my hand to press in deeply. I repeated this process several times until all the muscles under the skin felt smooth with no discernible knots. Then I moved to the inner lower leg and started all over again repeating what I had done on the outside.

The last part of the lower leg massage was to use my thumbs and finger tips to completely relax the big muscles in Samantha's calf. I must have worked there for at least five or six minutes until every muscles was soft and, again, there were no discernible knots. Then I lightly began circling my right palm around the back of her knee. This is an erogenous zone, and I continued this until Samantha reacted with another sigh, accompanied with a low moan.

Next I moved to the outside of her thigh. I took a long time to do cross-fiber followed by deeper, stronger strokes. This was capped with many long, slow strokes from the knee to the top of the pelvis on the outside of the thigh. I followed the same slow procedure on the back of the thigh. Samantha was obviously a runner. She had a lot of little knots in these muscles. It took a great deal of patience to find and smooth them all. When I found a troublesome knot, that resisted smoothing, I pointed my thumbs at it to soften it with an infusion of energy. Then a few massage strokes would release it. The only part of the leg left was the inner thigh. I slowly worked cross-fiber from the knee upward, moving very slowly. I went all the way up until my fingers lightly brushed the outer labia. Samantha made a slight movement and moaned softly at the contact. I continued these strokes from the knee to her pussy lips at least a dozen times. Each time I brushed the outer lips she would make a sound deep in her body, just the softest of sounds, but enough to know I was getting to her.

I then moved around the table to the other side and did nearly identical strokes on her right leg, including the dozen, or so, strokes at the end that included brushing against the entry to her most private parts.

I had purposely saved the buttocks until last. I started on the right cheek since that is the side of the table I was on. I massaged the entire cheek with slow, deep penetrating finger tips until I had covered the entire cheek. Then I switched to knuckles and continued to loosen the muscles. Samantha's buttocks were firm, not fat. They had a lot of muscles and some of those had knots in them, probably from the running. I patiently worked on each and every knot until it was as smooth as the rest of her. Then I went around the table and performed the same service on her left cheek.

The last technique I used on Samantha's back is for pulling everything together, to reconnect all of her body parts physically and energetically. I do this with several very slow strokes, the first starting at the sole of the foot and continuing up the leg, over the buttocks, and up the back to the shoulder. It is done firmly and very slowly. The second stroke is nearly the same except its path is up the sides of the leg with a pause at the top of the inner thigh to deliberately brush over the outer labia, then over the buttocks and on up to the shoulder. I do these strokes about four or five times. I usually lose count because I am focused on her breathing. Each brush with the labia elicits a moan and more restlessness with her hips. Then I switched to the other leg and pulled that side together with the same technique. By this time Samantha was definitely moaning and rolling her hips in reaction to the strokes at her pussy lips. I could tell she loved it. "Now it's time to roll over," I told her. "Do you want to be covered with the sheet while you are face up?"

She looked me in the eye and giggled, "No, I love this, and looking at the front of your shorts, so do you." She had me there. I was touting a nearly full erection, and there was no way to hide it in my shorts and t-shirt. I just smiled and told her to get comfortable, the best was yet to come.

She slithered, "slithered" is the only word that can describe it, into position on the table. I gave Samantha her next instructions. "Laying face-up is a vulnerable position for many woman. If you have unresolved trust issues, this is where they will surface most of the time. If at any time you get uncomfortable with a thought or emotion let me know right away. I will continue the movements that brought it up until they go away. This can be very effective if I get good, fast feedback. Otherwise, if nothing comes up, simply enjoy the massage."

She smiled and said, "I understand, and I promise I'll do as you ask. You don't have to be gentle with me. I seriously want to get rid of this baggage and this technique seems to be as good as any. And what the hell," she added, "if it doesn't work out, at least I can say I've had a really good erotic massage from the best." She smiled at me and closed her eyes, leaving me free to enjoy my first good look at her from the front. Her breasts were probably B cups, but her aureola were large dark circles accented by two beautiful, erect nipples that were easily the largest I had ever seen. I laid one hand on her abdomen and one on her right shoulder as I continued looking her over.

Her tummy was flat and the mons leading to her nether regions was prominent and covered with neatly trimmed, soft, curly hair that color-matched perfectly with the long tresses on her head. Her pussy lips were swollen slightly, but still fairly closed. I place one hand over her entire pussy, the other on her chest just below the collar bones. "Breathe in ... breathe out." I directed her, "Do it audibly like this," and I showed her. We easily matched our breathing and we continued this for at least five minutes, our breathing slowing noticeably every minute or so. "Let the energy flow from your pussy up your back to the crown on each in-breath, then on the out-breath see it flowing down the front of your body from the crown to your pussy. Once you have the vision in your mind, you only have to think 'crown' on the in-breath and 'pussy' on the out-breath." As I told her these instructions she began to get into it. I could feel the energy building in her body.

This woman had no idea what was coming. She was really good at this. Later I would have to ask her where she learned how to move energy like that. Finally I got what I was looking for. Samantha's pussy was beginning to move on its own volition in tune with her breathing. It was time for me to move to her hands and arms, and draw them into the mix. The procedure I used on the upper limbs was simply a shorter version of what I did on the legs, except arms are much smaller than legs, and it goes a little more quickly. I continued to massage at a very slow pace. I then brushed the palm of my hand with a feather light touch from Samantha's shoulder, across her breast, hip and leg, to her foot, saving the chest and abdomen until later. I started on her right leg and essentially repeated what I had done on the back of her legs. I added some extra work around the knee joints and was sure to bring all of the long strokes to the very edge of her pussy lips. Now Samantha's entire body was in tune. Every part of it was moving slightly when she reacted to me touching the sides of her labia. They were beginning to swell, filling with blood as she became more and more aroused. After I finished the second leg I moved up to her left chest. My hands began to massage all the areas of the left chest except the breast. I brushed against it from all sides at first, then I moved onto the breast itself, always avoiding the nipple. I was massaging methodically now, with my fingertips. I would drag them from the ribs up to within a breath of actually touching the nipple, then I would back off and do the same thing on a different part of the breast. She started trying to move so the nipple was in my path. I avoided her every time. At last I let my fingers brush the nipple and finally to gently take it and squeeze it as I pulled up and away from the aureole. I squeezed and twisted, pulled and released, and even gently blew cool air on it. Samantha began to moan. It was obvious her nipples were extremely connected to her genitals, because each time I squeezed, her hips would leave the table.

Finally, I leaned over and took the fully engorged nipple into my mouth and suckled like a baby, using my tongue to lick and press on it. Samantha began to thrash about. Before she had a chance to have an orgasm I stopped and just let my hand rest, palm down over the nipple as I moved to the other side and began the same technique on the right breast. This time it took her considerably less time to reach a highly agitated state. Again, I backed away. Then I moved to the head of the table and reached down to both breasts simultaneously. I began to rapidly squeeze and stroke her entire chest aiming most of my attention to those glorious nipples. In a very short time, I was rewarded with her first of many orgasms. She never exploded, but rather just seemed to slip into it gently as her entire body joined in the spasms. I held her breasts until she cooled some, then I moved to her abdomen.

After thoroughly working her upper and lower abdomen, I moved near her mons with a hand resting over each ovary, letting the energy flow. Earlier, when I massaged Samantha's legs, I left them spread apart where I had placed them to make them easier to reach. I was rewarded when I saw she had not drawn them together. She remained open to what was coming after. I treated my hands and her inner and outer labia with a generous amount of special oil I use for erotic massage. It is an edible oil that is slicker and has less texture than the jasmine I used on the rest of her. Again, I rested my right hand over her entire pussy and my left at her upper chest. We breathed together like this for a short time. I slowly let my middle finger sink into the groove between her pussy lips and slowly drew it upward just brushing across the top of the clitoris. I usually follow the same, or nearly the same patterns I was using on Samantha with everyone needing only minor variations due to feedback and sometimes body type. And there are literally dozens of different types of pussy shapes that require modification. I am happy to report that no modification was necessary for Samantha.

I started at her pussy hair and began to gently pull on it then release. I covered her entire patch several times. This was followed by squeezing her outer labia on both sides of her clitoris so it was literally compressing the clit into a small area. I held this for maybe a full moment before I released it. I repeated this several times. Then I did compressions with my thumb down the outside of one outer lip, between the lip and the leg, right in the groove. When that was completed I repeated it on the other side. Then I placed the fingertips of both hands on the uppermost part of the right labia and began to massage and squeeze the lip all the way to the bottom of the lip, almost to the perineum, the soft area between the genitals and the anus. Her body was really reacting by this time. Her moans were frequent and her hips in a continual state of movement, not large movements, but small movements that exactly matched the rhythm of my hands. When I finished the first lip I moved to the second. By this time Samantha's pussy lips were fully engorged and supersensitive. I grasped each lip in a thumb and two fingers and began running my hands up and down from top to bottom. Samantha's hips were now coming off the table as she tried to rise up to meet my hands.

Then I placed the index finger of my right hand against the clit and started circling it in slow soft motions. "Harder! Pinch it harder!" she urged through gritted teeth. I could tell she was nearing another orgasm, and I suspected it would be larger than the last. So I squeezed it, hard. "Arrrrrgghh! Oh fuck, oh fuck, oh fuck!" she shouted as her entire body tightened up and she flew over the top into a mind-blowing orgasm. Her pussy was flowing with juices and her body was vibrating all over.

Her eyes rolled up into her head and she was constantly keening shrill sounds and saying things like, "Oh fuck, oh yes, oh my God!" and other choice phrases. Her face had contorted so much she looked like someone else. And suddenly she let out a huge sigh and fell limp on the table. After a moment or two she looked at me with hooded eyes and smiled, "Thank you, I really needed that," she said.

I smiled back and said, "I hope you aren't thinking the massage is over. There is plenty more coming down the road. Just play there and be a good girl so I can finish my work." She chuckled at my word 'play,' but lay back and closed her eyes. I now had her complete trust. She was still splayed wide on the table. Her legs were spread nearly wide enough to do the splits with the knees bent so the lower legs stayed on the table. One arm was over her head and one beside her with the hand resting on her abdomen. My hands were still on her pussy, moving very slowly now, letting her continue recovering from her orgasm. I avoided the clit and spent most of the time on the outer regions of her outer lips.

Samantha was one of those women whose pussy had very prominent outer lips and almost no inner lips. When I could see she was back to Earth, I started in again. This time I used only my left hand to massage her clit and the lips around it. My right hand rested over the entrance to her vagina with my fingertips at the opening, just barely touching the entrance. I continued to wait. I knew that if I was patient her vagina would actually open to me and attempt to suck in my fingers. It took a while, but eventually I was rewarded. Her pussy seemed to be a vacuum and my fingers moved inwards, just the middle and ring finger. I slowly began to probe the fingers in and out, letting her get used to me being inside. I moved my left hand to her right breast and began squeezing and releasing the nipple. I could feel her body stiffen and she had another orgasm, this one small, almost an aftershock to what preceded it. Now Samantha began gently squeezing and releasing her inner muscles in concert with my efforts at her nipple. Then I curled my two fingers into a sort of hook shape and started doing come-hither motions at about one o'clock on the warm, moist inner wall of her vagina. She began to moan again, softly. After about a minute, I moved to the two o'clock position and continued, then on to the three o'clock position.

This continued until I reached the twelve o'clock position. Twelve o'clock was where I sought out the rough textured skin of the elusive g-spot. It was directly behind the clitoris. I gradually increased pressure as I did slow circles and come-hither motions on that part of her vagina. Her breath started coming in gasps and her body was moving violently on the table. I moved my right thumb to her clit and applied and released pressure in tune with my g-spot movements. I matched the rhythm of everything I was doing with my g-spot manipulations. I felt it coming just before it happened. Samantha literally exploded. Her whole body jerked and bucked on the table. She came and came, even squirting a little. I had never seen a woman squirt before. I was fascinated. Samantha's orgasm went on for several minutes and finally she collapsed on the table. She had fainted. I wasn't worried because I had seen others do this, but it was comforting to feel the heart beat and know she didn't just up and die from the intensity.

As Samantha began to recover, I couldn't help myself. I lifted her right leg high and slipped it over my shoulder. This left my mouth near her love nest. The aroma was overpowering. My senses breathed her in and I was instantly fully erect. I leaned my head in and began to lap at Samantha's juices. They were sweet and pungent and had a great taste. I love licking wet pussy and I found no reason to deprive myself. I pulled Samantha's clit into my mouth, gently at first, but as she responded I began to suck it in earnestly. It had grown and, as I sucked, it swelled with an additional blood infusion.

She was going wild again, and again I was rewarded with a strong orgasm. I guess she had a lot to make up for. As she came down from this orgasm I began running my tongue from bottom to top of her pussy, gathering in all the juices I could with each pass. After a few of these I pulled from under her leg and moved to the head of the table where I kissed her deeply and passionately, pushing my cum soaked tongue into her mouth in order to share her own taste with her. She really liked that.

"No one has ever done that for me before," she said. "I really like it. The only thing I can imagine would be better would be licking the juices off your cock after you came in me. Think you can arrange that?"

I assured her I could, as I lifted her in my arms and carried her to my bedroom. She was petite and well-toned, but in my arms that day she was like a feather. I placed her on the bed and before I could pull away she grabbed my t-shirt and began pulling it over my head. As soon as the shirt was off, I bent to drop my shorts and stepped out of them. "Now, let me look at you," she said. That made me a little nervous as her gaze intensified, but I must have passed because she smiled and pulled me down on the bed.

We were both so ready that no preliminaries were necessary. I had an erection that was probably the biggest I had ever had, and Samantha was soaked from the massage. I crawled between her legs missionary style and placed the head of my cock at her outer pussy lips. I moved it into the groove between the lips and moved it up and down a few times to get it lubricated, but the pre-cum probably made that unnecessary. Samantha reached down and guided my cock to her entrance. She looked me in the eye as I slowly sank all the way into her warm, wet passage. She smiled and said, "I hope you are ready because I am going to turn you every way but loose. I haven't felt this good about fucking a guy for a year and a half. I have a lot of catching up to do!"

With that said she began to slowly move her hips in small circles. I started gliding in and out to her rhythm. We continued this for a few moments, then the pace began to pick up until I was slamming into her like a jack hammer, every stroke going in to the hilt and coming out so only my cock head was still in. After several minutes of this I reached under Samantha's waist and without losing contact between us I rolled over and ended with her on top. She smiled as she grasped her new position of being in charge and brought her knees up high so we were connected deep at the groin. She sat there for several minutes, working her inner muscles. It was incredible! Her inner muscles were extremely strong. She would squeeze tightly, then release. The last hard squeeze she began to gyrate her hips in circles as she used her thighs to move her body up and down. I was going out of my mind. Then she reached down and grabbed both of my nipples and squeezed hard as she began moving up and down on my shaft while squeezing her inner muscles even tighter. That's all it took. I couldn't have stopped if I wanted to. I exploded deep in the recesses of her vagina. I spasmed three, four, five times more than normal! I wasn't counting, just letting my body go. I felt release in every part of me. Samantha stopped while all of this happened.

When I finally came down, I was in ecstasy. This is the point where my dick usually caves and begins to shrink and retreat, but Samantha had different ideas about that. She continued to knead its full length with the pulsing of her inner muscles. I was only allowed to get half soft before my erection began to return. This was a first for me. I never even knew it was possible. "Now it's time for me to get my wish," she said. With that she pulled off of me and kneeled beside my body while she bent low over my cock. She began to lick off the juices slowly, starting at the head and working her way down the shaft. Shortly after she started she swung a leg over my head and settled with her pussy less than an inch from my mouth. I was able to look at it and see our combined juices slowly oozing out and down across her mons. I touched the juices with my tongue. They were pungent and sweet. I pulled her hips slightly upward and buried my tongue in her pussy. I wanted it all. As she treated my dick like a lollipop I became ravenous wanting to lick up every single drop. I licked the groove between her pussy lips from her clit upwards to where the lips came together beyond the vaginal opening. Then I would go back to the starting point and do it again. Each time I licked her I paused to flick her clit several times as I passed. When she was finely clean I went to her opening and inserted my tongue and found more of the marvelous nectar.

Meanwhile Samantha had changed tactics. She was now breathing heavier again. Her moans were non-stop. Suddenly she exploded with another orgasm. I was so close I could feel the juices as they began filling her pussy. My cock became even wetter if that was possible. I stopped moving and just rested with my tongue still embedded in her hole. Finally her body began to relax. She rolled away. "Enough!" she said. Then, with a twinkle in her eye she added, "For now!"

We cleaned up in the bathroom, sharing a shower. We slipped on the robes I had available for clients, and went in search of food. We found Corn Flakes and milk in the refrigerator to start. Then we fixed a couple of hot dogs using the microwave. We both popped a beer and sat at the kitchen table to renew our bodies with the food.

"I feel wonderful! It's as if a huge black cloud has been removed from my stomach. I guess your technique is the best!"

I smiled and responded with, "I'm glad you liked the service. By the way, the best part is it's free! It's against the law for me to charge you for sexual services, so you aren't allowed to pay me. I never expected things to get out of hand like that. Hope you're okay with it." I was feeling a bit unprofessional at this point.

Samantha rose and came around the table to sit in my lap. "By the time you reached a point where you would have been breaking the law, I would have shot you for stopping. Relax! I loved it. It was just what I needed."

Samantha spent the night. When she left the next morning we promised to keep in touch, and we have. Sometimes we just go out to dinner, and sometimes we have mind-blowing sex at either her place or mine. We have become the best of friends, with benefits of course.

Chapter Sixteen

The Single Pearl

There she was with a group of people standing in the lobby of the Cromwell in Las Vegas as I was checking in. I noticed her single pearl anklet as I gave her an admiring glance from head to toes. She was a darker skinned small woman with a fiery green eyed look that could be very passionate I would guess. I could overhear the banter of the group, and her delicious laughter sounded much like a trickling stream of water in a parched desert, much like Las Vegas itself. A welcome change to be sure.

I fantasized about she and I meeting in the elevator as I was going to my room and we were alone. I saw her looking at me with a smoldering look, with a tip of her head to the side and downward. She had a twinkle in her eye as she was checking me out just as I was her. We smiled and faced the doors. Knowing I had only seconds to start up a conversation, I asked her if it hurt. She looked surprised and looked at me with a smile and a questioning look.

She asked, "Did what hurt?"

I smiled and said, "Did it hurt when you fell from Heaven?"

She paused for a second and then broke out in that pealing laughter, and asked if I used that line often? I answered, "Only when I am desperate." She laughed again and asked why are you desperate? I told her I knew I wanted to know her better, and I knew I only had seconds to get her to talk to me. She smiled and said well it worked and here we are. What now? I boldly asked her if she would like to help me find my room and check it out? She smiled and said well you certainly work fast when given an opening don't you? I said only when I am desperate, and then smiled. She looked at me thoughtfully and seemed to make up her mind.

She said, "Well, lead the way my desperate man."

I looked to see if she was kidding, and stepped out of the elevator at my floor, and she did too. I walked to my room number and she followed me. I unlocked the door and invited her in. She entered and then stood in the middle of the room waiting expectantly. I made a move and touched her arms, and leaned in for a kiss, and she tilted her head and leaned in also. As we kissed, she tasted so sweet and I wanted more. I touched her lips tentatively with my tongue and she opened her mouth so I could enter and touch her tongue with mine. Even sweeter inside, and I got lost in that moment, lost in the kiss. I touched her lightly on her back as I pulled her gently in to a closer hold and then let my hands slide slowly down her back to the top of her hips, and slowly pulled her to mold against me. She moaned lightly as she pushed against me to feel my erection already burgeoning against her stomach.

She asked, with a smile, "What do we need to do with that?"

I said, "Although we are two ships passing in the night, I would love to make love to you."

She said, "We have a very limited time as my husband will be looking for me soon"

I replied, "Perhaps he would like to join us."

And she said, "Perhaps the next time. For now I want you for myself."

"Absolutely!" I said, and she leaned in for another kiss. I immediately leaned in also to seal the deal. As I put my arms around her, I brushed slowly down to the hem of her dress and slowly pulled it up so her lacy leopard panties were showing, and I just knew her bra would match.

When she was just standing in her bra and panties set I stopped to just admire her beauty. I knew then I was right in thinking she indeed was a very passionate woman and I was in for a treat. I moved her gently to the bed and laid her down where I knelled in-between her legs, and just drew in the smell of her and her sexiness. I drew her panties down her legs and off over her heels. I leaned in and slowly rubbed my beard over her skin and down her lips, and then slowly ran my tongue out so I could taste her essence. She gasped with delight and began to moan very lightly under her breath.

I knew she would be sweet there also, and I was so right. She began to run liquid from her pussy as I licked it up. I knew she was keyed up and began to squirm delightfully as I went even deeper into her channel from top to bottom, and drew even more of her essence from her onto my tongue. As I licked her pussy, I looked up her body to see her twisting both her nipples with her fingertips, her eyes were closed and she was smiling. After she came again explosively and quit breathing for just a moment, she looked down her body at me and stretched languidly, saying, "That was amazing! You have to fuck me now!"

I of course said, "Okay!"

As I stood beside the bed and lifted her legs to my shoulders, and placed my rock hard erection against her wet slot of her pussy, and slowly drug the head up and down the slot to moisten my cock, I then gently pushed in. I waited a moment with just the head in, and then slowly pushed in the rest of the way. I gave her a moment to adjust, to listen to her sighs and then started to pull back. When I reached the top, as the head started out, I stopped and then pushed firmly back in and began to rock in and out to both of our delight. As she built to another climax I was heading down that road also, as her pussy felt like it had a dozen fingers inside of it. She squealed delightfully and asked me to cum in her pussy, and I had to let go and ride the wave along with her.

As we rested together, we kissed and I stroked her hair from her eyes and then suggested maybe we could have her husband join us the next time. She smiled and said he as well as her would love that. I asked how long she was staying in Las Vegas, and she said another four days. Just my luck, as I was there for the following four days also, but then again, I guess that will be another story.

Chapter Seventeen

Why He Craves MFM Experience

For her to enhance her playtime and elevate her sexual energy and pleasure to a whole new level.

To see her enjoy sex from a different view that can't be experienced from one on one.

Our sex life is so much more often, intense and enjoyable, since we started enjoying sharing with other participants.

To give her the ability to have no hang ups about sex with herself and with her body.

To see her mind and soul be satisfied in a way with pure raw sex that can't be achieved in one on one.

She desires to have more than one man at a time and, for me, to be able to share that with the woman I love is amazing.

It is simply so exciting to share her with someone nice and share the sexual experience of them sharing each other with me.

I can't perform as long or as well as I would like and she needs more to satisfy her sexually completely.

It is so hot seeing them orgasm together, especially him bareback and knowing she has welcomed his climax into her. Then me making love with her after she has been so sexually satisfied.

I simply love the feeling of my wife's pussy after she has given herself to another man. The smell, taste and feel of their cum in her pussy is the most exciting and pleasurable feeling one can experience.

I could go on forever why we both enjoy inviting another man to share our sex time to please my wife together.

Chapter Eighteen

Why She Craves MFM Experience

To be with two men brings a feeling that plainly cannot be brought through one on one.

The rush, the erotic mood, the inhibitions that fall to the wayside, the total release of the mind and body to bring me to a place that I cannot get enough of.

Sharing this time with my husband staring deep into his eyes while another man is deep inside of me, the thoughts of how much I love him for allowing me to do this runs wild through my mind, making me so much more horny, causing me to explode with multiple huge drenching orgasms.

To have that different sexual experience each time with someone different, and sharing that new excitement with my husband.

Well, just because sex with multiple men is so much damn fun!

It is so exciting to flirt with another man, knowing how attractive he finds me and knowing how badly he wants and desires me.

It turns me on just to think about it.

Chapter Nineteen

I Was The Anniversary Present

We met a couple and she and I seemed to click more than our spouses did. I was asked to meet her at her house and plan on spending the night with her. This was our first night away from each other in 45 years, except for hospital stays. To say I was a little set back was an understatement.

We made the arrangements and the day arrived. I went to her house and found her alone. I asked where her husband was and she said I was her anniversary present. She was allowed to spend the whole night with me alone. Wow, was I surprised! We had a few drinks to settle down and she was dressed in a sexy negligee with an awesome thong underneath! I was hard as soon as I saw what she was wearing!

She was nervous and we both giggled a lot. After sipping our drinks and going to the bedroom in the basement, we snuggled and kissed and hugged a lot, with music in the background, with the candles and darkness encompassing us.

I was flattered beyond the realm of believing. I just knew someone was going to pinch me at any moment, and I was going to awaken and find it was only an erotic dream! I began to slowly undress her, and each piece of clothing revealed her brown and soft and sexy body. I kissed each exposed piece of skin as it was revealed, enjoying not only the feel but the taste and smell and texture of it. I looked into her smoldering green eyes and thanked her for choosing me and allowing me to be a part of this adventure.

I placed her in the middle of the bed and moved immediately south to where I knew her smoldering center was waiting for me to show her what I knew about pleasing the woman's body. I tentatively leaned down and rubbed my face over her mound to smell and savor the juices I knew would be there. I was surprised that there was very little smell or aroma, but the juices were indeed flowing like a fountain. The taste and sweetness made me want more. I licked from bottom to top of her slit, and was rewarded with an ambrosia of sweetness only an excited pussy can give. One lick and I was there for the evening. I slowly swiped my tongue along the sides of her major and minor labia along with the center to capture the juices seeping from there. Her clit was hidden and gave me some difficulty making it come out to play. It was okay, though, because I do enjoy the hunt for the clit. I was successful in my endeavors I'm proud to say, as her clit did come out to play. She was moving about the bed and moaning and pulling my head into her center to make sure I was going to stay there. Like I was going to leave! There was just too much fun there! She came repeatedly from my oral administrations and then demanded I fuck her right away!

I stood at the side of the bed in my favorite position so I could thrust that much harder into the center of her pussy, and she quickly slid to the corner of the bed and I began to slide my cock up and down her slit to wet it, to get it ready to insert it into her pussy! She began impatiently moaning and rubbing up and down my cock and finally begged me to fuck her! I slid in slowly, as my penis is a little thick.

When I was seated deep as I could go I waited so she could get used to me being there. When she began to move her hips up and down, I knew she was ready to begin. I began to move in and out and kept lengthening the stroke until I was pulling out, until the head was at the edge of her pussy and going as deep as my balls would allow with her legs on my shoulders. I held her feet to each side of my face and rubbed them on my face as I kissed and sucked her feet as well as her toes. She came quickly as this was a new experience for her, and was excitedly erotic, as it was her first time. As she was moaning, I was stroking as hard as I knew how. Her pussy was like velvet gloves stroking my cock deep within her. As she came, her pussy would tighten and grip me almost to hold me from moving inside her.

She kept begging me to cum in her pussy, but I knew from past experience that I was generally one or two and done for the evening, but if I delayed it I could go all night from the edge. I would stroke her slow then fast, and then pause as she would cum again and again from the different speeds and thrusts, and directions my cock would go. She finally asked could we rest and cuddle as she was tired and sensitive from cumming so much. I of course agreed, as a delay always is a good thing for an all-nighter. We lay upon her bed as I asked her to tell me the story of how we got here in the first place.

She recounted to me that I was her anniversary present from her husband, and she was to call him at some point in time in the evening to speak to him and recount her adventures of the evening. I asked her if she wanted to do that now and if I needed to leave the room? She said she would, and I did not need to leave. I listened to her end of the conversation as she recounted to him what had transpired thus far. What an ego builder! I would recommend it to any man as it is so cool and exciting to hear the conversation from another point of view! I told her I was flattered beyond measure, as this was the only time this had ever happened to me in my lifetime.

She said she thought I would make a good lover for her, and it was a good time to test the waters. We snuggled and kissed as only lovers can do, and I rubbed and stroked her as I am a massage therapist, and unconsciously rub women the right way. We talked and recounted our meeting of the four of us in the hot tubs and pools at the resort, with our first meeting of the four of us and the outrageous flirting and heavy petting of the two couples with each other's spouses each time we met. We also commented on the several times we met and explained the lifestyle as we saw it from our perspective to the both of them as a couple.

I asked her what she wanted from that evening's experiences and she said she had already warned her husband to be careful unlocking Pandora''s Box, as it would not willing be closed again. She said he had been after her to do this for ten years, and she finally wore down and said okay, but be careful what you wished for! Truer words have never been spoken by a woman or a man!

We rested for awhile and I continued to stroke and pet her in all the right places, and she began to respond which told me she was ready to begin again. I moved south to where I love to be between a woman's thighs, and began to lick and kiss lightly her major and minor labia searching once again for the elusive clit she had. I so loved her light taste and smell as I rubbed my face against her mons and pussy, and licked and stroked her pussy to get her to cum for me! I rubbed my fingers up and down her slit to loosen and lubricate her center and then pushed my center finger up till I felt the roof of her pussy, and felt the rough patch there, which told me I had found the promised land of her orgasms! I continued to rub there a little at a time, and then built up till I was rubbing briskly back and forward until she came and shuddered and moaned, and thrust her hips into the air and finally begged for a moment to gather herself as her orgasms were quickly overtaking her ability to think or breathe. She squirted then, and did not even know it! She had never done that before.

After she rested, I asked her if she had ever squirted before, and she said she had never done that. I proudly informed her that she had indeed done that now! She denied it and I showed her the bed sheets to prove that it was so. She seemed to be embarrassed, and I told her not to be embarrassed, as it was a point of honor for anyone who could make that happen, as that was a true milestone all women strive for! I was the one who achieved that with her and I was indeed proud of my achievement!

After we rested, I started to rub and stroke her once again and she responded and began to moan and twist her hips as an international sign she was ready to breed. I once again went to the corner of the bed and she knew by now what that meant, and met me there on the corner. I raised her thighs onto my shoulders and again slid my cock up and down her slit to moisten the head of it to ready it for its journey to the center of the depths of her joy. She began again to move her hips up and down to try to get my cock to enter her pussy yet again. I paused and then thrust to her center as hard as I could and the air left her lungs in a whoosh of surprise! The look was priceless as she looked on in wonder as I began to forcefully stroke her center as deeply as I possibly could with as much force as I could give her. She started to moan and cry as she began to cum repeatedly from the assault I put upon her. She then began to thrust and beg me to fuck her as hard as I possibly could, and then she began to squirt repeatedly on my cock as I did as she requested.

After soaking the bed sheets and both of us, we began to cum together and then collapsed onto each other to regain our strength and breath.

Several times during that night we found ourselves wrapped around each other and desiring more. We fucked off and on until, finally, at six thirty in the morning we used my morning wood to fill her pussy for the final time together! I cleaned her up after the sex to cement our relationship together. We showered together afterwards and went to breakfast at the Waffle House, and she took me back to the condo at the resort, back to my wife. I recounted what had transpired to my wife and she and I fucked again to recommit our love to each other, as we always do when one of us spends time with another person alone.

Chapter Twenty

Judi and Others

We were at the pool at the resort one day and we noticed a handsome man sitting on the other side of the pool from us. He seemed to be watching Judi very closely, as only a husband can observe. I told Judi.

As usual, she said, "He was not!"

I told her he was interested in being with her and she of course said, "No he wasn't!" I told her I would prove it to her and she asked me how. I said I would ask him if he wanted to fuck my wife. She said, "You won't do that."

I said, "Really? Watch."

I asked him if he would like to spend some time with my wife, and he laughed and said sure he would! I then told her it is on. I told him I would wait here and he should bring her back when they are done. They laughed and went up to the condo while I waited at the pool.

About an hour and a half later they returned and he personally thanked me for a great time with her. She smiled and also said it was all good. We then went to the condo and got in the bed and she told me all that went on, as I pleasured her pussy to get it ready for me to be the second man she had that day. She said he wore a rubber and described what they did and she came repeatedly as I ate her the whole time she was telling the story, as it seems to excite her to tell me what went on in my absence. I of course could not taste anything except her cum, as he did wear that rubber. It was still delightful, as it was exciting to her and I thrive on her excitement as well as mine. Of course I had to gloat and tell her I told her so!

We went to the corner of the bed after I had eaten her to many squirting orgasms, and placed her legs on my shoulders so I could once again reclaim my bride. This was the beginning of countless times she and Steve, and many other men would be together over the next four years as their paths would cross. Many times she would tell me she was going to go up to the condo for a little bit and see me later, and I would wait and watch as she would go with different men and enjoy their sexual prowess in various ways so she could share them with me later, as we once again reclaimed our love for each other.

The sight and smells of the before and after of the chance meetings are what I thrive to enjoy. To have the rare opportunity to share with the three of us together is a blessing in itself as only a true voyeur can understand.

Chapter Twenty-One

Happy Wife, Happy Life

I decided to sit down and share how I was lucky enough that my wife agreed to try being a "hot wife." Let me start by saying, I never thought it would completely change how we lived our life or that it would make us both so happy. My wife gave me everything I asked for and so much more. My name is Jerry and my wife's name is Judi. When I first wrote about this, we had been together for about six years and married for four years, with no children. We were both in our mid-thirties and both of our backgrounds had been the usual monogamous relationships. But we happened to have an amazing relationship and we were always pretty open and honest with each other before Judi became a "hot wife," although I would say that we were completely open and honest with each other. Our sex life had always been strong and neither one of us ever had any complaints. Judi is 5' 8" tall, has long brown hair, nice D sized tits, a few extra pounds with curves in all the right places (as she would say), and a very pretty face. I think most men would consider her a trophy wife and she could honestly probably have any man she wanted. She is extremely modest and is critical of herself probably to a fault. I would describe her as being on the conservative side, but she does have an adventurous and outgoing personality. I am definitely a lucky guy to have her as my wife.

When I was single and in my early twenties, I had the pleasure of having a couple (who were in their thirties) move into the apartment next door to me who turned out to be swingers! After getting to know each other and becoming friendly, I was invited over and that turned into us getting together on a regular basis for threesomes. We actually became pretty good friends, while of course I and her husband had mind blowing sex with his wife. The way they talked and interacted with each other was different from any couple I had ever known before. His wife loved fucking me and he loved having me fuck his wife.

It completely changed my perspective on relationships, and ever since then I knew I wanted to have that in my own personal relationship, but good luck finding the right one! I would laugh at how hard it was to just find a girl for a simple compatible relationship, never mind adding swinging to the mix! I had told Judi about my experience with this couple after we had been dating for awhile, and felt comfortable telling her. Judi took it pretty well, commenting on how it must have been a lot of fun for me, and asked what sorts of things we did. Of course I tried to contain my excitement when telling her about the amazing encounters, but I made it clear that it was fantastic and I really did like it a lot.

Judi, being the detail orientated person she is, asked me if I meant the sex or the swinging part. I told her both, and tried to discuss the subject with her. Judi agreed that the sex part sounded very hot and she did listen to my attempts for us to try it, but she would always say that she didn't want to go there.

Over the years, I would always try and bring it up at times, to try and open the door. I looked at it like it would only enhance our sexual relationship to a higher level. For example when we would be out having a good time and I would see a guy flirting with Judi, and see that she enjoyed innocently flirting back, I would comment about it later and ask her if she would want to have sex with the guy. She never got insulted and she would say that flirting is completely different than having sex with someone.

Well, I finally started to see a subtle change in her response about my commenting when she didn't shut the door on it, but would just smile at me and start to kid with me that I was funny and kinky. I thought there might be hope.

Finally, when we were on vacation, I got a more positive response. We were out having some drinks and we had met this couple who we were talking to. It turned out that Judi had agreed to play pool as his partner, while I stayed at the bar with his wife, as we were going to take winners of the game. I watched them playing their game and saw the guy she was playing with and the two guys they were playing against checking out Judi's ass as she bent over for a shot, and there was no doubt that she knew it and was having fun with it. At one point, I'm not sure who initiated it, her partner was standing behind her with his arms reaching around and showing her how to make a shot. She was sticking her ass out and rubbing right into him. Later that night, when we got back to our hotel, I of course teased her about it and her response was different this time.

Judi asked, "So you really wouldn't mind if I had sex with another man?" I told her that I would actually like it if she did, but we should probably set up some rules if it were to ever happen. Judi inquired, "What kind of rules?"

That turned into a discussion that lasted for hours, and my important rules were basically safe sex and not getting emotionally attached. The result was that Judi confessed that over the years she had thought about my many attempts to bring up the subject. She said that the more she thought about it, the more it definitely turned her on, that she could have sex with my permission, but she told me that she didn't see herself ever being okay with me fucking another girl. I let her know that I was okay with that and she was surprised. She always thought that I was trying to get her to go along with swinging as I wanted to be with another woman. I explained that if she ever allowed me to have sex with another woman I would gladly accept. But I also told her that I was absolutely fine to just be with her, and that I would love for her to be a "hot wife."

Judi responded, "A what?" I laughed and told her that a "hot wife" is a married woman who has permission to have sex. Judi laughed and said that she had never heard of such a thing, and joked that she wasn't all that hot, but was married. I assured her that she was hot and I would love for her to try it.

We had been drinking for hours at this point and Judi posed the question, "You've had too much drink, let's see what you say tomorrow morning?" I of course already knew the answer to that and couldn't wait for the morning.

The next morning came and while we were still in bed, I quickly reminded her of our conversation, and that I would really like her to be a "hot wife." Judi laughed at me and started to tease me by talking to me in a sexy seductive voice. She started saying some of the dirtiest sexy stuff I ever heard her say up to that point, while she was stroking my cock. I was hard as a rock! I had never heard her talk like that or even thought she was capable of saying such dirty things out loud. I would say the dirtiest things I heard her say to that point in our lives was, "Fuck me harder!" or, "Your cock feels so good!"

Our sex was always great, but it was just regular sex. She was now saying stuff like, "So you want me to kiss another guy and let him put his hands all over me, finger my pussy, slide his tongue up and down my pussy and then fuck my pussy?" She could see that I was turned on and loving what she was saying. She then told me to show her what I wanted another man to do to her. I must have spent about the next hour doing everything except fuck her. Then I fucked her good.

Afterwards, Judi said, "Holy crap, you really do want me to fuck another guy!" I reminded her that I've been trying to tell her that all along and wished I would have clarified earlier that I was okay with her just doing the fucking. I will never forget the next moment. Judi was looking at me and she made a big exhale. She told me in a dead serious tone, "I will fuck another guy for you if that's what you really want."

I got instantly hard by her just saying that to me and I lifted the covers up to show her. She was laughing and asking if that happened from her telling me that, and I said, "Yup." She was still laughing but she started telling me how we could have a lot of fun with this. I felt like I just hit the lottery or something. I had been trying for years to hear what she was now saying to me! Now she was talking to me with excitement about all the possibilities and different ideas. She surprisingly told me about three guys she knew who always flirted with her and she was sure wanted to fuck her. One guy owns a restaurant that we always go to, another guy worked at a deli she goes to, and the other guy was a mutual acquaintance of ours.

I joked with her how she knew that there were three guys who wanted to fuck her and that proves that she is "hot." I was also a little surprised about the owner of the restaurant, since we eat there all the time, and I never saw him hitting on her. Judi explained that every time she picks up food to take home, he comes over to her and hits on her. A couple of times he didn't even charge her for the food. She also admitted that she does get hit on all the time, which I already gathered, but those were the only guys that she would consider as of now.

I asked Judi if she liked one of the guys in particular and she said that each one was cute and seemed to be nice, so that wasn't an issue since it would only be sex. Judi told me that I would have to decide which guy she should fuck. I still think about her saying that to me from time to time. I actually gave it some thought and I couldn't help but think to myself how I was not only going to pick the guy to fuck my wife, I was going to be making one of these guys very happy, and they had no idea. I told her the guy at the deli sounded good.

His name was Alan and we agreed that she could go out for some drinks with him and see how it goes from there. I joked with Judi that it was the best vacation I ever had. Judi contemplated, and said that when we wrote our vows for our wedding years back, I should have included, "Do you promise to fuck other men for your husband?" I laughed at the thought and told her that I would have, but could you imagine the priest's face if I did? We had a good laugh at that. I told her that I could ask her now if she wanted me too. Judi was also laughing and even dared me to ask. I composed myself and seriously asked her the question.

Judi then got serious herself and answered, "I do." It was now official, and we laughed and hugged each other at our unofficial "hot wife" ceremony.

After we got back from vacation, Judi wasted no time. The first night after being back she told me that she had set up a date to go out with Alan the following Friday night. We had sex every night that week, often talking about it. During that week, she also went on line and apparently looked up everything she could about a "hot wife." I guess I didn't really know all there was about it, because she filled me in on the many different aspects of it. We actually talked about it in depth and what things were on the table and off the table.

As I said, Judi is very detail orientated. We both enjoyed talking about the subject, and I have to say that she was very interested in this new found topic. She also told me that she read about a cuckold being part of a "hot wife." Neither one of us had ever heard about a cuckold in our lives! We talked about it and honestly I wasn't sure about it, but talking about it with her did seem to turn me on. Surprisingly to me, Judi told me that she found the idea a turn on too. She explained that it seemed like a sexual power thing and she would like to experiment with it. She asked me to think more about it, which I told her I would. She basically told me that she wasn't really sure yet as to why it turned me on, but she broke it down by telling me that if it turned me on as much as I said it did, and I wanted her to do it, then that's what she would do.

Secondly, she told me that she had always wanted to experience more men sexually, but always hesitated because she didn't want to ruin her reputation. All her life she only had sex with the guys who she dated, which was a total of five including me, plus a one night stand with a married guy once. Her thoughts were that she wouldn't be able to find a good guy to marry if she had a reputation of being a loose girl. But then, since she was very happily married and secure, and since I wanted her to experience more men on top of it, she pretty much felt that it's a no-brainer! "It makes sense to me," she said. She emphasized that making me happy was her first priority.

She also broke my chops in good fun at how she was a pretty lucky girl for me to ask her to have sex with others, while I could only have sex with her. That Friday came and she was definitely nervous, but excited about the evening to come. After she got home from work, she took a shower and then asked what I thought of her shaving job. She had shaved her pussy in the usual manner, which was bare except for a little patch of brown hair just above her lips. I gave my approval as I tried to start playing with her, she shut me down and told me that I had to wait for that. She told me to help her pick out an outfit, which I wondered why. Judi told me that she would not fuck anybody unless I was an active part of it. She told me that she wanted me to experience it with her, even if it was not sexually. I liked how she had actually given it some thought, while I was just thinking about the sex part. I chose a short dress with no panties and high heels. I have to say that she did look hot. She finished doing her hair and makeup, then she gave me a kiss and said that she would give me a call later.

Before she left, I told her that I had given some thought to the cuckold style and I would like to try that as part of the "hot wife" thing. I pretty much told her that I would leave it up to her how she would want to experiment with it. She was happy to hear that, and then she teased me on the way out the door saying, "Wish me to have a good time!" and I did just that.

A couple of hours later, Judi called me and said that everything was going great and she was having a good time with him at a bar about a half hour away from where we lived. She also told me that she had already kissed him and he had fingered her in the car when they got to the bar. She let me know that it would definitely happen and asked me if I was sure that it was what I wanted. I assured her that I did and told her to have fun.

About an hour later, Judi called me again, this time from the bathroom, and told me that she was going to leave the bar with Alan and go back to his place, where she had left her car. She told me that she would give me a call when she was on the way home. I asked if she was going to have sex at his place and she said, "Honey, I'm not here for the beer, that's what you want, right?" I told her it was, and to enjoy herself.

She laughed at me and told me that she was sure that she would. We hung up and I can't tell you how turned on I was knowing this was going to happen. A couple of hours later, I got a text with a picture of Judi's pussy. She wrote, "Freshly fucked for you, babe!"

She had never sent me a picture of her pussy before, and as I was staring at it, my phone rang. It was Judi. She asked what I thought, and I told her how hot it was and that I loved the picture. She let me know that she would be home in twenty minutes. I went back to the picture and admired her pussy. It glistened from the cell phone camera flash and her lips were red and swollen from the apparent fucking she had just received. I could see that she took the picture in her car and she had spread her legs open to take the picture while she was wearing the short dress I picked out. I also remember sitting there with my heart pounding, and I don't think I had ever felt so turned on in my life. Having my wife tell me that she just fucked another guy and she even sent me a picture as proof, was just incredible. My cock was as hard as a rock and dripping pre-cum like I pissed my pants. I couldn't wait for her to get home.

Judi got home and she immediately kissed me roughly. It was like she was a dog in heat. I was a bit surprised at how aggressive and turned on she was. Don't get me wrong, she gets turned on when we are together, but she was undoubtedly turned on beyond what I had ever seen. I asked if she liked it and she said, "Yes, I fucking loved it! Okay, now show me how much you loved it!" We dove onto the bed and I lifted up her dress and started eating her out. I could smell an odor of rubber on her pussy, which I knew was from the condom that covered Alan's cock when he fucked her. I let Judi know that I could smell the rubber and she went on telling me how he ate her out and fucked her, while I continued eating her. As she was giving me the very detailed account of how she got fucked, she had to stop talking to cum. She had never cum from me eating her out before, and I knew that her orgasm was a result of her reliving the fucking that she had just received. I asked if he had made her cum and she said, "Yes, once." She also let me know that his dick was a little smaller than mine, but he knew how to use it very well. We then had sex, which lasted for all of about a minute! Thankfully, I barely even got soft and we kept fucking for about another hour until I gave her my second load. Afterwards, we talked about how amazing it was and Judi told me straight out, "I want to do this again!" I couldn't agree more with her.

I asked if she would feel comfortable if I could join in as a threesome, and she told me that she would think about it and see how it goes. She explained that she wasn't sure if Alan would go for it. Alan knew that she was married, but he thinks that she was just fucking around. I commented that I guess that meant she wanted to fuck Alan again, and she said, "Well, you said I could fuck right?" I of course said yes and reminded her that it would stop if either one of us wanted it to.

She laughed and said, "You didn't think I would enjoy it this much, did you?" and then let me know that she would of course follow our rules and thanked me for talking her into it. She also confided that the simple fact that I allowed her to do it was a major turn on for her. She said just knowing that I had that much faith in her to have sex with others, with me having full confidence that I would not lose her, was almost better than the actual sex. I did confirm what she felt was true, although I kind of joked with her that I didn't really think it through like that when I asked her to try it. I was glad that she felt that way about me and also that she really enjoyed the sex. I was looking forward to it being a regular thing.

Judi fucked Alan I think like three more times at his place and we always had awesome sex when she came home. She would always be very detailed in telling me exactly what she did with him and I loved it. One time, she even called me and left the phone next to the bed so I could listen to her getting fucked the whole time. She also told me that Alan not only loved to eat her pussy out, but he would also lick her ass. She said that he liked it when she got on top of him in a 69 position so he could eat both her pussy and her ass! Judi told me that it was a little weird at first because she never had that done to her, but now she really enjoys it and wanted me to do it. Needless to say, I have been licking her ass ever since. I will say that Judi is impeccably clean and I don't think I would ever do it with another woman.

Alan also fucked her in a position, one that she had never tried before and she really liked. Also, needless to say, we use that position ourselves now. After what I think was the third time she fucked Alan at his place, she let me know that we were going to have a threesome. She went on to explain that she told Alan that her husband knew all about her fucking him and he got a little nervous. She told him that it was okay and that she had a high sex drive that her husband couldn't keep up with, so we had an agreement that she could fulfill her needs as she needed. She told Alan that she always wanted to have a threesome and asked if he would try it. Alan agreed.

Judi invited him to our house and he showed up right on time. We had some drinks and I could see that Judi was very comfortable with him. After about a half hour, the uncomfortableness between me and Alan was gone and we got along great. Judi came out of the bathroom wearing a very hot negligee that had two holes in it so that her tits hung out. She suggested we bring it into the bedroom, which Alan and I didn't argue with! We went to the bedroom and as she started kissing Alan while I got undressed, and then I started feeling her up. Judi turned her attention to me and began kissing me. Alan then got undressed and he was playing with her pussy as Judi and I fell onto the bed on her back. I slid my hand down and felt that Alan had already unsnapped the crotch of her negligee and I started fingering her along with Alan. Judi stopped kissing me and I could see that she had her eyes closed and was enjoying both of our fingers inside of her. I started sucking on one of her nipples as Alan settled in on the other side and was sucking her other nipple. We both kept fingering her. Judi had one hand on each of our heads, holding us in the position of sucking on her "girls," as she calls them. Judi was rotating her hips as we both continued fingering her and it wasn't long before she tensed up and came on our fingers. I was loving every minute of watching her enjoy having two men. She got up onto her knees and pushed Alan to his side as she began sucking his cock without saying a word. I saw that she had her ass up in the air with her legs spread wide as an invitation. I got behind her and slid my cock up and down her wet lips, then delivered Judi my naked cock. She was on birth control and our rules were that if she fucked anyone else, they would have to wear a condom.

As I pounded her from behind, I could see that it was interrupting her rhythm on sucking Alan's cock. I slowed down a little so that she could concentrate better on sucking him. Alan was lying there and had propped a pillow under his head, just watching her suck his dick. After a while, I asked Alan if he wanted to fuck her, which he nodded in approval. I tapped Judi's ass and told her to switch. Judi complied and was sucking my cock as I laid down and she kept her ass in the air for Alan. I watched Alan move in behind her, put on a condom, and he was pounding her in seconds. I was glad to see that Judi had taught him well and he was compliant with our rules. Judi stopped sucking me and was just holding my cock as she enjoyed Alan.

She had her eyes closed and was resting her head on my leg. She was facing me and she had her mouth wide open as I could see she was thoroughly enjoying Alan fucking her. I laid there and watched Alan fucking her. It was the first time I ever saw Judi getting fucked and little did I know that it was the first of many times! After several minutes, Judi pulled away from Alan and she straddled me. She faced me as she guided my cock into her. She sat down on my cock and then pulled Alan towards her. He was kneeling next to her and she started kissing him with an open mouth as she held his head with both of her hands. Judi was riding my cock and kissing Alan while moaning lustfully. I couldn't believe how turned on she was. It was like she was in ecstasy. Judi broke away from kissing Alan as she let out her orgasm moan. I love feeling her pussy cum when I'm fucking her. The best way I can explain it is that it goes from having your cock sliding in and out of a nice wet pussy to sliding in and out of a lake. It's just a flood. I wasn't long behind her when I released my own cum into her, as she put her arms around Alan and held onto him as I was cumming. As I finished, Judi raised off of me and laid down on her back next to me. She opened her legs and said to Alan, "Do you want to fuck my used pussy?"

Alan replied, "Mmm, don't mind if I do!" and kneeled down between her legs. I got to watch him slide his cock right inside of her as he held her legs in the air and started fucking her. I couldn't believe that she said that to him, but I loved it. Judi grabbed my head and pulled me toward her mouth. I kissed her as I could feel her body move with each thrust from Alan. She was moaning as she kissed me and I could feel my cock getting hard again. We kissed the whole time Alan was fucking her and I held onto her tits as they were bouncing with every thrust he gave her. It probably took about five minutes for him to cum, and, after he pulled out, he went down and ate Judi for a couple of minutes. I didn't say anything, but I was thinking to myself that he knew that I had just blown my load in her, so he was eating my cum as well.

Afterwards, Alan asked us if we wanted him to hang around, but Judi told him that it wasn't necessary. Judi thanked him and told him that she would be in touch. I also thanked him for coming over and I hoped that he enjoyed himself, which he let me know that he did, while thanking both of us for the invitation. Alan left, and Judi and I laid on the bed next to each other reliving our first threesome of many to come. I told Judi that I couldn't believe she asked Alan to fuck her used pussy, and I commented on how aroused she was. She let me know again that she had no idea of why or how it turned me on to see her get fucked by another man, but she was glad that it did.

As far as the comment to Alan, Judi told me that she started talking dirty to Alan when she was fucking him at his house and he liked it when she does. She apologized for not letting me know that she had done that with him before. I was taken a little off guard and wondered aloud why she didn't talk dirty to me during sex. Judi laughed at me and said, "You know how sex is kind of unique to who you're with." She gave the example that her boyfriend she was with before me liked it when she fingered his ass while giving him a blow job. I would never have thought Judi would have ever done that. I was intrigued by how much I was now learning about my wife and that she was obviously capable of being much dirtier than I had always thought. I inquired how she knew that Alan liked her to talk dirty. Judi explained that it was easy. She told me that the second time she fucked him, he started joking with her that she was a little married slut who needed to get fucked. She knew he wasn't joking and he really liked the idea of her being a married slut who wanted to get fucked by him, so she started telling him that was exactly what she was. I guess Alan and I had a lot in common, because I got hard again just listening to her say she was a married slut.

I let her know and she laughed saying, "Yeah, I already figured that part out when you told me I could fuck other men, honey!"

She let me know that she hoped that I didn't change my mind and I continued to allow her to fuck as she wanted. Although she reminded me that she is not okay with me fucking another woman, just in case I had any ideas of that happening. I laughed and assured her that I was not only happy that it added to our sexual relationship, but that it was also satisfying to her.

Of course I also brought up how Alan had eaten my cum out of her afterwards, and Judi said that she was also surprised. She said that she would ask him about it and if he liked how it tasted. We both agreed that it was very hot. I teased her a little about not getting attached to Alan, since I could see that she really did enjoy fucking him. Judi assured me that it would never happen. She confessed that when she first started thinking about doing this, she decided that she would look at any men who she fucks only as toys. She explained, "It will be just sex and nothing emotional, kind of like my dildo." I laughed at how she looked at it and told her that I wanted to fuck her used slutty pussy. Judi smiled and started talking really dirty to me. We went for another round of sex and we loved it.

Afterwards, Judi told me that if I wanted her to be a real slut then she would have to fuck more men than just Alan.

I didn't even have to think about it and told her, "I want you to be a slut!"

Judi said, "Oh, I will, I just hope you can handle it," and kissed me goodnight. I thought about whether or not I should include the next part of our journey, being that it was not good. But, anyway, I decided to include it, since it was a part of our experience, so here goes. About a week after our threesome with Alan, Judi told me that she ran into the mutual acquaintance she had told me about, and his name was Buddy. She asked if he was interested in discreetly meeting for a drink and he agreed. I helped her dress up before going out with him as usual, and she would keep in touch with me to let me know how it was going. She let me know that they had a few drinks at a nearby hotel bar and everything was going okay, and Buddy had gotten a room for them. About a half hour later, I got a call from Judi and she was upset. She told me that she was on her way home. I pressed her about what was possibly wrong, and she said she would explain when she got home.

When she got home, she told me how everything was fine when they went up to the room. They had some foreplay and then Buddy started fucking her doggy style, when he started to get rough with her. He pushed her head down onto the bed and held it there forcefully while he fucked her. He spanked her ass hard and the side of her leg to the point where she was in pain. She was telling him to stop, but he continued doing it. She told me how he kept saying to her, "Shut up and enjoy it!" Well, she finally had enough and turned around and punched him right in the face giving him a bloody nose. She was then able to get her clothes and get dressed. She said that he was asking what was wrong with her. She kept telling him that he was an asshole and then she left. Needless to say, I was pissed off and wanted to go find Buddy myself. Judi calmed me down and told me how it was one of those things that can happen. She explained how we both thought he was a normal nice guy, but sometimes you just don't really know someone until they are in a certain situation. She believed that he thought it was normal to be rough like that with a woman. Afterwards, when she was calling him an asshole, he was sitting there totally calm and asking her what he did wrong. I told her that maybe it wasn't a good idea to keep doing this, and I was surprised that Judi talked me out of it. Judi told me how it was okay and there are bound to be bumps in the road.

We joked with each other how she was now the one trying to convince me that she should be able to fuck other men. We both chalked it up to a learning experience and the only thing that I found to be positive out of what happened was that there was absolutely no doubt that Judi wanted to continue to be a "hot wife," even after a horrible experience like that.

The next week, Judi invited Alan over and we were back to having another enjoyable session of sex. Before he came over, Judi had let me know that she asked him about when he ate her out after our first threesome. She said that his answer was that he loved doing it and that he would like to do it every time if we didn't mind. Judi and I both found that to be a huge turn on and agreed that he should clean her up. When Alan got there, we jumped right into having sex with Judi, who was dressed very sexually for the occasion. I had let

Alan know while he was in the middle of fucking Judi that I loved Judi being a little slut. Alan opened up, while still fucking her, and told me how ever since he had gotten together with Judi, he hoped that he could find a girl who would be just like her. He told us how he would love to have a wife that was a slut. I teased Judi, "See how I'm not the only guy!"

Judi told Alan, "I am your slut," and he would have to keep fucking her, even if he found another girl. Alan apparently liked what she was saying because he came seconds after! As soon as he pulled out, I slid my bare cock into Judi and it didn't take long for me to fill her up. I looked over at Alan and asked if he was ready to clean her pussy. Alan said that he would clean it good and then I pulled out. Alan planted his mouth on her pussy, and I watched him suck my cum out as Judi moaned with pleasure.

Afterwards, Judi joked with us that she didn't know what all this slut stuff was about and joked that she was having an identity crisis. She asked me if she was a "hot wife" or a slut. I laughed and said apparently you are a married slut to Alan, but you're a "hot wife" to me. Alan was cracking up listening to us and asked if Judi had any sisters! I also couldn't help but think how Alan was then experiencing what I had the pleasure of when I was around his age. I knew that one day he was going to be begging his wife to be just like Judi.

When Alan left, Judi and I talked about our encounter as we usually did. I asked her if she meant what she said about being Alan's slut and he would have to fuck her even if he found a girlfriend. Judi told me that she really enjoyed having sex with Alan and wanted it to continue. She explained that it was important to her that she satisfied him, especially since she wanted him to keep fucking her. She said if he liked me being his slut, then that's what I'll be for him. She asked, "Did you see how quick he came when I told him that?" I understood what she meant and let her know how happy I was not only for the unbelievable sex that we were then having, but also that she was really enjoying her sex with Alan too.

Judi said that she would like to keep Alan as a regular for sure, but she also wanted to find other men to fuck on more of a once or twice basis. She even joked that we might have to hold off on having children for a while because this was way too much fun. Judi also brought up that Alan had asked her if she wouldn't mind shaving her pussy completely clean because he liked that, and she asked me if I would mind. I actually like some hair, which she knew, but I gave her the go ahead since I also knew she wouldn't have asked me if she didn't want to do it for him. She gave me a big kiss and told me that she would alternate months. She said she will alternate shaving it clean for a month and then I can have it however I liked it for the next month. I told her I wanted a full winter bush so that when Alan ate her he would think of me when he got a hair in his mouth. She laughed her ass off and said that she liked that idea!

Judi also asked me if I would be okay with letting Alan cum inside of her if he got tested for STDs and was clean. She added that she really does love it when Alan licks my cum out of her and would love it if I would clean his cum out of her. I let her know that I would definitely give it a try. Judi called Alan not a second after I finished saying that and he said he was making an appointment the next day to get the test done!

A few weeks later, Judi told me that she was going to go out with her girlfriend for a few drinks. She said that she would like to try and get picked up by a guy and asked me to help her pick out an outfit that I thought would help make that happen. I chose a tight pair of jeans with a half shirt and a sexy thong that revealed itself when she bent over or sat down. We agreed that she would take off her wedding ring so that she could pretend to be single. She headed out and I sat home with anticipation, waiting for a call.

After a few hours, Judi texted a picture to me of her arm around a guy and asked me if she could bring him home. I let her know that if that's what she wanted, then absolutely. I was a little surprised that the guy didn't seem to fit her usual taste in men. He was Spanish looking, with a full beard, and shorter than her. She texted me back that I was her brother and I was staying with her temporarily. I should be pretending to be asleep in our spare bedroom/office when she gets home. She told me that I would have to listen to her getting fucked, and she would leave our bedroom door open in case I wanted to try and watch. I answered back, "Okay, sis."

Judi pulled into the driveway, followed by this guy she picked up. I was in the spare bedroom and they came inside trying to be quiet, but they were anything but quiet. Judi was saying that she thinks her brother was asleep. I could hear that they made it to our bedroom, and I snuck out into the living room, which is just outside the bedroom door. There was silence as I figured they were kissing at that point. About ten minutes went by when I heard the first moans. Judi was moaning loudly and I figured it would be safe to peek in. They were both completely naked and this guy was between Judi's legs eating her pussy. Judi was looking right at me and discreetly waved to me with a smile. I smiled and waved back. When he started to come up from eating her, I ducked back to the couch. Minutes later, I heard the unmistakable sound of skin smacking against skin. It sounded like he was pumping her like a machine gun. I peeked in quickly and saw she had her legs up in the air, while he was lying on top in the missionary position. His ass was pumping up and down like a jackhammer. I ducked back onto the couch and listened to Judi screaming out, "Oh yeah, fuck me harder!" and she was screaming so loud that I wondered if she was doing it on purpose to drive me crazy or if he had a huge cock. He didn't last long. It was over in less than five minutes. Shortly after that, I heard rustling around and I headed back to the spare bedroom. I heard the front door open and Judi telling this guy to drive safe on the way home.

When the door closed, I came out of the room and Judi met me in the living room completely naked. She took my hand and led me to our room. I got undressed and she picked up the used condom off of the nightstand. She laid down on the bed and held up the condom to show me the huge puddle of cum that was inside. She asked if I was proud of her and I told her I would be prouder if she swallowed all that cum. She smiled at me and asked if I would really like that. I told her to let me pour it into her mouth, to which she just said, "Mmm."

I grabbed the condom and she opened her mouth. She held her tongue out and I slowly drizzled the cum out onto it. I couldn't believe how hot it was. After I drained it all out, she told me to kiss her. I didn't even hesitate. We kissed like never before with our tongues intertwined. I still couldn't believe how turned on we both were while we enjoyed this guy's cum in her mouth. It got me thinking dirty and I actually surprised Judi a little bit by talking dirty to her during sex. I was telling her what a good whore she was and telling her that I liked that she couldn't get enough cock to satisfy her. It was kind of a heat of the moment thing, but to my surprise, Judi really got into it and was answering me with things like she can't help being a whore and she hoped that I still loved her. All I could say was, "Oh my God!" it was that good. It was another amazing night of sex. Afterwards, we talked about everything and she let me know that she really liked how I talked to her and wanted to hear it more often. She told me that she used to be such a good girl and now she loves being a bad girl. I told her that I loved her being a good girl, but I would have to say that I love her even more being a bad girl! I let her know that I couldn't be happier. I also let her know that I had thought about what she said about me cleaning Alan's cum out of her and I wasn't sure if I would like it or not, but now, after kissing her with another guy's cum in her mouth, I had no doubt I would love sucking Alan's cum out of her pussy!

Judi just smiled at me and said, "Yes you will."

About a week later, Alan called Judi to let her know that he got his report back with a clean bill of health. Judi invited him over that night to celebrate. Alan certainly loved fucking her bareback, because he came in about two minutes. After he pulled out, I got down between her legs and I watched a steady stream of his cum ooze out of Judi's pussy. I admired it for a few seconds and then scooped up a nice puddle onto my tongue and fed it to Judi. We kissed each other with pure passion as we enjoyed coating our tongues with Alan's cum. It was incredible. I then went back and finished cleaning her up for about ten minutes. I then slid my throbbing cock into her and blew my load in about three seconds.

Alan then licked her pussy clean. After Alan left, Judi came over to me and kissed me for about fifteen minutes, telling me over and over that she loved me so much! She told me that it was a huge turn on for her to have me clean Alan's cum out of her and vice versa. She commented that we must really love her pussy to suck each other's cum out of her. I let her know that I definitely do love her pussy and I would love to clean out cum from any guys that she let fuck her. Judi told me that from now on she wants her pussy cleaned all the time, even if it was my own cum.

About two months before then, Judi confessed to me that she had always been attracted to her boss and wondered if I would be okay if she tried to have sex with him. I told her that I was fine with it if that's what she wanted. She had worked as an office manager for this dentist named Wayne for about the last ten years. She said that they have always had a professional relationship and there was never any flirting, ever. She asked how she should try to approach it and I told her to just start flirting with him and telling him how good he looked or something. I figured that if he knew that she wanted him, there was little to no chance that he would turn her down. I knew him pretty well, since he has been taking care of my teeth since we got married. He was about twenty years older than us and Judi told me that he had been married for about thirty years. I also knew that Judi knew his wife pretty well and I asked her if that bothered her. Judi surprised me by telling me that she would not feel the least bit guilty about disrespecting his wife in any way. She explained to me that she is a stuck up bitch, thinks she is above everyone else, as all she does is drive around in her Mercedes all day and go shopping. She never worked an honest day in her life, and she talked to Wayne like he's incompetent. She added a few other unpleasant thoughts about her, but that's the gist of what I remember her saying. I never knew that Wayne's wife was like that, and I had to say that Judi never talked bad about anyone, so I was pretty sure she wasn't exaggerating.

I asked her if her dislike for his wife had anything to do with wanting to fuck Wayne. Judi told me that primarily she had just always been attracted to Wayne, but it would be satisfying to her for

Wayne to come to her for his sexual needs instead of his wife. She also said she was pretty sure that his wife didn't satisfy him sexually, and he deserved to have a woman who satisfied him and treated him with respect. I asked how long she had felt this way about him and she said ever since she started working for him.

I loved that she was honest with me about her thoughts and feelings, which I knew would never have happened if we hadn't agreed on doing this "hot wife" lifestyle. I did question if she thought it was a good idea getting involved with her boss, which she assured me that she could handle that part of it. Well, the next day after our talk, Judi came home and told me that it was easier than she thought it would be. She explained that she commented all morning on how nice he looked and gave him the "come fuck me" eyes, as she calls it. At lunch, she asked him if he found her attractive and he said he thought she was beautiful. She told him that she was embarrassed, but let him know that she had a high sex drive that I couldn't keep up with, and hoped that he might be able to help satisfy her. She told him that she had talked to me about asking him and I would also really appreciate it if he could help out in satisfying her. She said he didn't even have to think about it, saying of course he would help! She said he would be coming over the next night after work.

The next night, Judi asked me to help her pick out something to wear for him, and we agreed on a negligee that she looked like a high class hooker in. It was complete with thigh high stockings, high heels and all. She greeted him at the door in her outfit while I sat on the couch. I heard him say, "Oh my God, you look gorgeous!" She led him into the living room, and I shook his hand and thanked him for coming over to take care of Judi for me. He said no problem at all and was joking with me that he had never realized how gorgeous Judi was. He kept saying how beautiful she looked and how he loved her outfit. My guess was that Judi was right about his wife and he probably hasn't even seen an outfit like that in a long time. Judi quickly dragged him into our bedroom. I stayed in the living room to wait and see if Judi would let me come in and hopefully join in.

About ten minutes later, Judi yelled out for me to come inside, and, when I did, Wayne was already sucking on her tits. Judi told me that Wayne was okay with me watching if I wanted to. I grabbed a chair and sat down to watch. I have to say that, for an older guy, he was in pretty good shape and he fucked Judi well. He came when Judi was riding him, and Judi immediately took off his condom and poured out his cum onto her tits and rubbed it into her skin like lotion. She even sucked his cock clean. Afterwards, Judi praised Wayne at how well he fucked her and kept thanking him up and down. Wayne said he was glad to help out, and Judi then asked me right in front of Wayne if it would be okay with me if they could have sex anytime they wanted too. I gave my permission that they could fuck as much as they wanted, and whenever they wanted. Wayne said that he would like that, especially since his wife only has sex with him once every six months or so. Judi was dead on with her assessment. She acted surprised though, and told Wayne that it looked like they could both help each other out with their sexual needs. I vividly remember her saying to him, "My body is yours whenever you want it."

Wayne opened up a little bit and was telling us that he couldn't believe it when Judi told him about wanting to have sex with him. He kept telling Judi how gorgeous she was, even though he was finished fucking her, which made me giggle to myself that he must really mean it!

Wayne was asking us if he was on Candid Camera or something, which we learned was an old TV show where people were tricked while being secretly recorded. We all got a good laugh, and we explained to Wayne that it sounded like the show, "Punked", which he never heard of, by the way.

A couple of days later, Judi called me during the day to let me know that she was going to stay a little late after work to fuck Wayne in his office. She picked up dinner on the way home and told me about her office sex while we had dinner. She also told me that she had talked to Wayne about being STD free and Wayne assured her that he was clean. He said that he would love to have unprotected sex with her. We discussed letting him cum inside of her without getting a test done, as we both felt comfortable that it would be safe. Judi said she couldn't wait to have all of us cumming in her regularly. I joked that she would probably have cum from at least one of us inside of her almost every day of the week, which she replied, "Mmm."

I reminded her that not all that long ago, I was trying to convince her to just have sex with one guy! She asked me what I thought about the idea of having at least one of us fuck her every day for an entire month so that she would have fresh cum in her every single day. I told her I thought it was a great idea and she said after her next period was over, she wanted to do it. Just the thought of that got us so hot that we had sex on the kitchen table! Afterwards, Judi asked me if I regretted asking her to be a "hot wife," which I assured her that I had no regrets. She was happy to hear my answer and just wanted to be sure that she wasn't taking it too far. I did let her know that when I asked her about doing this, I never in my wildest dreams thought she would fuck like this. I mean we always had sex regularly, but it was like she turned into a complete nympho. I also told her that when I asked her to try out being a "hot wife," I was thinking that she might have sex with a guy here and there, and, hopefully, we could try doing some threesomes, but she had obviously taken it to a different level. She admitted that she had no idea she would like it that much and didn't really care what the label would be. She actually said to me, "I think I'm more of a married slut at this point." She explained that I can call her a "hot wife" if I want, but that was just a nice way of saying it. She explained that she really liked the idea of having three men dedicated to only having sex with her, and she was going to ask both Wayne and Alan if they would commit to only fucking her! I didn't think that would be fair to them and she said maybe she could say that she would probably allow them to fuck someone else as long as they asked her permission. I thought that sounded better and teased her that I might ask permission, which she quickly reminded me that the answer would be, "No!"

The following week, Wayne came over and Judi gave him the good news about not having to wear a rubber. Apparently he liked it, because he came over almost every day that week after work. Judi cuckolded me a few times that week and made me watch Wayne dump his loads in her. I noticed when watching them together that there was a definite connection between them. She didn't fuck him like she fucks Alan. I knew there was feeling behind it and I questioned her about it. Judi confirmed my suspicions and admitted that she does fuck Wayne with feelings and was pretty sure that Wayne loved her at this point. She assured me that she could handle it. She explained that he had always been good to her and he was the nicest, most respectful man. She said that their sex had definitely exposed feelings for both of them, but she said it made the sex even better. She kept assuring me that she could handle it and I was fine with that. She also said that she had talked to Wayne about having me joining them, and Wayne agreed that he would be okay with me joining in.

By the end of that first week of enjoying Judi bareback, Wayne gave Judi an extra week of vacation, a $15,000 raise, and a $200 a month cash allowance to be used for buying lingerie. I was ecstatic, needless to say. Judi said that Wayne told her he really enjoyed being with her and he had never had better sex in his life. He also wanted Judi to know that she deserved the raise he was giving her, and it was also a small way to thank her for making him feel so alive again. He added that if Judi decided she wanted to stop having sex with him, she would still keep the raise, extra vacation and even the extra monthly cash allowance!

Judi was completely shocked and she even talked to me about not accepting anything from Wayne. I was like, you can't be serious? Well, it turned into a huge argument, which is rare for us. The money part really bothered her the most. She truly wanted nothing more than sex with him. She argued that she was happy with what she already gets out of it, which is Wayne simply having sex with her! She loved it and didn't want or need anything more.

I was able to convince her that he was only giving her all this extra stuff as his way of showing his appreciation for, as he says, "Making me feel alive again." I argued how we could use the extra money to take an awesome vacation every year along with the extra week of vacation. I also reminded her of how he said she would keep the extra perks and money regardless of whether the sex continued or not. Thank God he said that, because that was what tipped the scales for her to finally accept it. One thing I learned without any doubt from this argument was that Judi not only liked having sex with Wayne, but she wanted it. Deep down I knew he was going to be a permanent sex partner, which I was okay with.

The first day after her next period was over, Judi reminded me of her plan to get filled with cum every single day. All I can say is that it was a great month, LOL. Judi literally had either Wayne, Alan or me fuck her every day and on quite a few days she even got multiple loads of cum! I was literally eating either my cum, Wayne's cum, or Alan's cum out of her almost every day. I say almost, because Alan helped out and she finally started making Wayne clean up his own cum!

During that month, we started doing threesomes with Wayne also. On the last day before her next period, I asked her if she would arrange to have Wayne and Alan to come over one after the other so that I would be able to enjoy cleaning up after all three of us. She arranged for Wayne to come over and after he deposited his cum, she called Alan to come over. When Alan got there, I fucked Judi and deposited my cum, and then Alan finished her off by depositing his cum. We had Alan leave right after and I got to enjoy sucking all three loads of cum out of her pussy for about an hour. Her pussy was a wet sticky mess and we both loved it. I even put one last load in her for the month and cleaned that up too. We talked about the whole month afterwards and I let Judi know that I didn't think she would ever be able to top what we had done. Judi said she loved it too, and for the first time in her life she was happy about getting her period, just so she could have a break. I thought that was the funniest thing. She proudly informed me that she got fucked a total of thirty six times between the three of us in twenty eight days! She said she was trying to count the number of orgasms she had, but lost count. She estimated that it was about sixty!

She also proudly commented that she didn't think there were many married woman, if any, who had ever experienced a month of sex as she did. I figured she was probably right, as she almost always was. At different times when fucking Alan and Wayne during the month, Judi also accomplished her goal of getting them to commit to her. I was there when she asked them, and Wayne said he had no problem committing to her for sex, and said that he even might have to ask permission once a year to fuck his wife just so she doesn't get suspicious.

We laughed our asses off and Judi told him that she could live with that. Alan promised not to fuck anyone if Judi could take care of him at least three times a week. Judi agreed to their terms, but reminded Wayne that he can have her as much as he wants and whenever he wants. Judi said that she plans on being honest with Alan and Wayne about her little harem of men. She wanted to let them know that she was regularly having sex with the three of us, including what the terms are, so that everyone will be on the same page. She wanted to have Wayne and Alan meet and hopefully once everyone was comfortable with each other, she could choose different combinations of threesomes, and also have all three of us devour her all together every once in a while!

If you are wondering, she did ask me if I would be okay with all of that, which I didn't think there was any need saying what my answer was! There was one night during the month of her getting fucked every day that sticks out in my mind. I was working a double at work and I found out from Wayne that he stopped by the house to see Judi. It was about 10:30 p.m. when I got a bunch of pictures sent to me and they were from Wayne's phone. He texted, "Just left your house. I thought you might enjoy some of the pictures I took." He sent me pictures of Judi kissing the head of his cock, sucking his cock, his cock in her pussy, her sitting on his cock posing for him, and a bunch of others. I told him that I loved the pictures and asked how long he fucked her. He said for about two hours, but didn't tell Judi that he had taken a Viagra.

I got a laugh out of that and told him he better cough up some of those for me if he wants to keep it a secret. He promised he would. When I got home at 11:30 p.m. I asked Judi how the night was and she said, "It turned out to be a lot of fun." She explained that she had been sexting with Alan all day while at work, she stopped by his apartment on the way home from work for some sex and figured it would be a quiet night, but then Wayne stopped by. Wayne told her that he wanted to take some pictures of her, so she posed for him, at first wearing different underwear and outfits, then he took pictures and videos the whole time they had sex. She commented that it must turn him on to take pictures because they fucked for two hours. I just laughed and kept my secret safe with Wayne.

Wayne would come over to the house regularly two or three times a week, and Judi would also take care of him at the office sometimes. It was funny sometimes when I asked how the day went at dinner, because she would be telling me stuff and then say, "… and Wayne fucked me before we left," or, "… I gave Wayne a blow job after lunch," like it was just another thing during the day, LOL. There was one night that I got a text from Wayne asking if Judi was home. I said that she was, and asked if he was coming over. He replied back that she wasn't answering her phone and he wanted to stop by for a quickie. It turned out that Judi had left her cell phone in her car by accident. I told him that I would have her ready for him in five minutes.

I then told Judi that Wayne was coming over for a quickie and I needed to get her ready. Wayne showed up about ten minutes later and I had her waiting in our bed, naked with her legs open, and with her dildo sticking out of her box! I asked Wayne how that was for service, and he said that he was going to call me from now on when he was coming over! We had a good laugh at that.

She also kept her promise to Alan and fucked him at least three times a week. Sometimes she would go to his apartment and sometimes he would come over to our house. She usually left it up to Alan if he wanted solo or to include me, but sometimes she would just tell him straight out that I would be joining in, because either I said I wanted too or she was just in the mood for it. She even cuckolded Alan for the first time and I loved it. She made him sit there and watch me fuck her, and afterwards she picked up her thong, wiped up my cum out of her pussy with it and threw it to him. She told him to take it home, sleep with it on his pillow, and maybe she would think about fucking him the next day if he was good. Alan was confused, but he didn't argue with her. He just said okay and took her thong home with him.

The next night she did take care of him over at his apartment. When she got home, she was all smiles and I wondered what she was so happy about. She told me that she will be cuckolding Alan on a regular basis from now on. I of course asked what she meant, and she explained that he was extremely submissive to her when she went there and was wondering if he did something wrong. She said that she jokingly told him that she just wanted to make sure that he obeys her, and that turned into him telling her that he will do whatever she tells him to. She said that he even got very submissive during sex, but she quickly corrected him. She told him to keep fucking her like he had been, but other than that he had to obey her. Alan promised that he would.

Judi then told me, with a devilish smile, that she wanted to cuckold Wayne the next night. The next night after work, Wayne came over. She got him naked and sat him in the chair next to our bed. She put on a stripper like show for him to tease him. She even hovered her pussy over his cock like she wanted it and when he tried to put it in, she would pull away telling him he can't have it, while teasing him by asking him how much he wanted her and stuff. He was completely sexed up after about a half hour of her doing this to him. I was even aching to fuck her just by watching it. She told him to stay in the chair and watch me fuck her. While I ate her out, I kept telling Judi how good her pussy tasted in order to drive Wayne even more crazy! And, after I got done fucking her, Judi told Wayne to, "Come over here and clean Jerry's cum out of me!" Wayne jumped out of the chair and was eating my cum out of her in seconds!

I could see that he was getting really turned on by her moaning. She was asking him if he liked how she tasted and he was saying, "I love it, I love it!" over and over in between sucking on her pussy. There was no doubt in my mind that he really did love it by watching the way he was frantically eating her out. After about fifteen minutes, Wayne got up on his knees and when he was just about to stick his dick in her, she pushed him back and told him to just rub the head of his cock up and down on her lips.

He did exactly as she said and every time he tried to stick it in, she would loudly say, "No, I didn't say you could fuck me!" She kept teasing him like that for about ten minutes, and then asked me how it felt fucking her pussy. I knew exactly what she was doing, so I told her that it was the best pussy in the world, and it always felt amazing. "Why don't you let Wayne feel it, you know he would love to be inside of you right now?"

She asked Wayne if that was true and he wanted to be inside of her, and he said, "Come on, you know I do, I will say please, Do you want me to beg you?"

She then told him, "You will do what I tell you to do, now go home and think about that." She gave him a kiss and said she wanted to hear his answer tomorrow.

Wayne was saying, "Are you kidding me?"

Judi told him dead seriously, "Do I look like I'm fucking kidding? Do what I tell you!" Wayne had the same confused look that Alan had and I tried not to smile. Wayne got dressed and left shaking his head. I was asking Judi if she knew what she was doing, because I didn't really want to take the chance of pissing off her boss. Judi told me not to worry because there was no doubt that Wayne would submit to her and she just wanted to establish that she was in charge. She asked me how it felt helping her cuckold him and I had to admit that I liked it.

Judi laughed and said, "At first I felt kind of bad doing it, but now I fucking love it, in case you haven't noticed." We were both laughing at that point and I confirmed noticing how much she liked it. She further explained that she was going to have to reward Wayne when he submits to her, so I should pick out a negligee for her to wear to work under her clothes. I picked a nice blue one she had and hoped that she knew what she was doing. She said that she was certain that he would submit sometime during the day at work, and it would be important that she rewarded him immediately. I had never seen this dominant side of her in all the time I have known her, but I have to say that I liked it.

The next night after work Judi got home and she had that confident smile like she did after cuckolding Alan. I took a guess that Wayne submitted to her and she rewarded him. She smiled and said, "I told you he would." I asked how it went and she said it was great. She explained that he asked her the very first thing in the morning if she would stay after work to talk, and she said she would think about it. By lunch time, he was pleading and begging her to stay. She agreed and gave him a quick peek at her negligee. He told her to cancel the last appointment and closed the office early to be with her. She said she was soaked all afternoon and couldn't wait to fuck him.

Judi told me that he said he would do whatever she told him and that he loved her. She said she told him to get on his knees and say it again, which he did. She said that she told Wayne that she loved him also while he knelt in front of her, but she will never leave me and that it would only be sex between them as long as he did what she said. She asked him to respect that and if he understood. He told her that he understood completely, and he promised that he would respect that. She said she even told him that she would have to remind him of his obedience from time to time. After that, she said they had sex from three to five o'clock, and he fucked her twice, adding that he cleaned up his cum both times! She said that in the middle of fucking her the first time, he kept promising that he would do anything she wanted with no questions asked.

I asked what she said back, and she said she told him, "I know you will baby." She said the funny thing was that it looked like he really gets off on being told what to do. She explained that as he was saying that to her, he started fucking her really fast, and when she answered him back that she knows he will, he exploded inside of her. She said she even commented that it really looked like he liked being told what to do. He told her that he would only do what she told him to, and went right down to clean his cum out of her. After that they kept playing with each other until he got hard again, and that led to the second round. She explained to me that she thought it was amazing at how she has so much power over him now. She went on to say that Wayne is very dominant as long as she's known him and likes to have control with almost everything. She said if she was single and fucking him, there was no doubt in her mind that she would be on her knees obeying whatever he told her, but for some reason when I cuckolded him it turned him into being completely submissive to her.

I could see that she was very happy with the situation, maybe gratified might be a better word, but the fact was that she loved it. I was a little concerned that she told Wayne that she loved him. Although, quite frankly, I already knew it. I was kind of relieved to hear her say that she made it clear that she wouldn't leave me, and it was only sex with him, but I did bring up what we originally agreed to, that she wouldn't get emotionally involved with anyone. It was a long conversation, but the bottom line was that she satisfied my concerns and she could keep it under control. I also brought up my suspicions that Wayne may become a permanent sex partner in our marriage.

I let her know that I would be okay with it if she wanted it, and the result was that she would want that, but me being "okay" with it was not enough. She needed to know that I wanted it too. I knew it would mean a lot to her and I told her that I did want it. She told me that I would have to tell Wayne that it was what I wanted, which I promised to do.

I truly love how my wife was. I love that she was constantly getting fucked and even more so that she loved it. The one thing about her is that in everyday life she is the most proper, well-spoken, and seemingly conservative woman you could ever meet, and you would never guess she had her own harem of three men to service her sexually. She still asked me what she should wear for Alan and Wayne, and sometimes even asked me if there is anything that I want her to do with Alan, or if I forbid her to do something. The best example of that was one of the times when Alan came over, I told her that her pussy was off limits from being touched in any way. Alan used a little KY and slid right into her ass while I watched. Afterwards, she reminded Alan of his duty and he cleaned her ass while she stayed on her hands and knees. She asked Alan if there was anything off limits for me, and Alan said I couldn't touch her pussy either. Then I fucked her ass, and I didn't even need any lube.

After I was done, I told Alan to clean her up and he got right in there. At one point, Judi said she would try and push some out and to get ready. I couldn't believe how much cum she pushed out and she had cum farts, where there were literally white bubbles forming around her asshole from all the air that was trapped in her ass from the fucking! I wish I had it on video. Judi said her ass was sore for the next two days, but she said it was worth it! I definitely wanted to do it again and get it on video next time to show her what it looked like.

To bring it up to date, Judi let Wayne know that she has been having sex with Alan and was honest about what her arrangement was with him. She even let him know that she had threesomes with Alan and me regularly. She told Wayne about it after fucking him at our house one night, and Wayne did not have a problem with it. Judi let him know that Alan got tested for STDs and he was safe. She also told him that she wanted him to join in having threesomes with her and Alan. She said that Wayne asked her if she was asking him or telling him. She said that she was telling him that he would. He just said, "Okay."

Judi assured him that he would like Alan, and would arrange it so that they could meet at our house before doing anything. As for Alan, she told him about Wayne and what her arrangement was with him. She also told him that she wanted to have a threesome with him and Wayne, and that she would invite him over to get to know Wayne a little beforehand. Alan was completely on board and even told Judi that she should play with all three of us at the same time. Judi let him know that it will happen, but she wanted him to meet Wayne first so that Wayne would feel comfortable.

Two days later Judi had Wayne and Alan come over to the house. We all had a couple of glasses of wine and Judi was wearing one of her sexy outfits while she flirted with us the whole time. She explained to Wayne that she shaved her pussy one month for Alan and let the hair grow the next month for me. She also let him know that she would maintain it however he wanted the next month for him. Wayne requested a neatly trimmed strip of hair, which I was happy to hear. Judi thought it sounded like a good compromise for all of us, and asked if we would all be okay if she just kept a strip of hair all the time.

We all agreed that it would be good. After about forty five minutes of conversation, I could see that Alan and Wayne were comfortable talking with each other, and Alan even said he was going to make an appointment to get his teeth cleaned! Judi and I gave each other a look of approval, and Judi came right out and asked Wayne what he thought about Alan. Wayne said he thought he was a very nice guy and liked him.

Alan said the same thing about Wayne. Without wasting another minute, Judi then told us all to follow her to our bedroom, where she told Wayne that she wanted him to watch me and Alan fuck her. We all got naked, and Wayne sat down in the chair next to the bed and watched me and Alan go to town. Alan and I worked Judi over as Wayne watched and I could see that Judi was more verbal than usual. We spent about an hour devouring her, and she made Alan cum while she was blowing him. She pulled his cock out of her mouth and jerked his cum out onto her face. Watching that made me bust my nut inside of her.

When I pulled out, Judi told Wayne to come over and clean her dirty pussy. Wayne buried his mouth into her pussy and Judi was wiping the cum out of her eyes and licking her fingers as Wayne slurped up my cum. Judi grabbed my shirt and wiped the rest of the cum off her face and told me and Alan to bring our cocks over to her. We knelt on each side of her while she alternated sucking our cocks back to hardness. We were both hard in no time. I went down and told Wayne that I would give him a hand eating her and we alternated eating her pussy, while she enjoyed sucking Alan's cock. After a while I told Wayne to lie down and Judi to get on top of him. Judi started riding him and I got behind her. I told Judi to slow down and I was going to give her my cock also. It's something I always wanted to do and she did too. I got my cock inside of her pretty easily and she now had her first two cocks in her at the same time!

Unlocking Pandora's Box

Alan was kneeling next to her and she was trying to suck his cock, but not doing a very good job. The next thing I knew, I heard Wayne letting out some gasps and I felt my cock sliding a lot easier. I knew that Wayne had just shot his load. That got me so fucking turned on I shot my second load, which was more intense that the first one! Judi rolled off of Wayne onto her back and was saying how incredible that just felt. I agreed with her and asked Wayne what he thought. Wayne said that it was the first time he ever did that in his life and he loved it. Judi told him that it was a first for us as well, and asked Alan if he had anything left. Alan happily accepted her invitation and was on top of her in seconds.

Wayne and I watched Alan fuck our pussy for about ten minutes when he finally shot his load. He cleaned her up immediately after he was done. I said, "our pussy," because at this point Judi's pussy belonged to all three of us, without any question. Alan and Wayne left soon after that and we talked about our first foursome and first double vaginal. We both absolutely loved it and couldn't wait to do many more of them.

The next night Wayne and Alan came over and it didn't take long before Judi ordered us to get naked and sit on the side of the bed next to each other. We all sat down and she modeled herself in front of us wearing nothing but a thong, asking if we liked what we saw. We were all complementing her and then she sat down in between Wayne and Alan. She asked Wayne if he remembered saying that he might need to ask permission to fuck his wife every once in a while, which Wayne acknowledged that he did. Judi said, "Well, I want you to fully commit to only fucking me for the next six months, can you promise me that?"

Wayne didn't even hesitate saying that he would definitely commit to that, and at that point he didn't really care if his wife got suspicious if he didn't ask her for sex. Judi just said, "Good, then we can talk about it again in six months."

Judi then explained that since we were all committed to only fucking her, our cocks now belonged to her. She told us that her only rule was simple, "Nobody touches your cocks except for me, and if I get the feeling that you violate that, then you will never fuck me again, understood?" Wayne and Alan both agreed, and I of course said that she already knew my commitment.

Judi then explained that she was dedicating herself to the three of us for the next six months. She actually said, "I will not fuck anyone but the three of you for the next six months, and all three of you now own my pussy." She explained that either one of us can have her at any time, either solo or with any combination of the other two. She also said that if she desires one of us or any combination of the three of us, then we would give her what she wanted. She said, "It will basically be like I'm your slut and you're my boyfriends."

She went on to say that she wanted open communications between all of us and she also thought it would be nice if we hung out together without her sometimes, and then come home to her. She went on to say that there was nothing off limits as far as sex goes, but she didn't want to go out to dinner or anything with Wayne or Alan without me. She said, "I love you guys, but my heart belongs to my husband and this is just about sex."

She did explain that if I wanted her to go out for dinner or drinks with one of them alone, then she would consider it. Judi asked us if we were all in agreement and we collectively all agreed. She then got a big smile on her face and said that there was one more thing. She told Wayne and Alan that she and I wanted to video tape all of us fucking her and asked if they had a problem with it. Wayne and Alan didn't object, and Judi told me to make sure that I make copies for them of anything we tape. She thought it would be pretty hot for us to take turns videotaping each other fucking her, and maybe make our own little porn collection! We all liked the idea of that. Judi then told me to turn the camera on, so I went over and turned on the camera, which I had set up on a tripod. She got up, took off her thong and said now let me start taking care of my cocks.

Judi went over to Alan and told him that she wanted him to feel how wet his pussy was. Alan rubbed his fingers along her pussy and then started fingering her. She then moved over to Wayne and told him to feel how wet her pussy was. Wayne followed Alan's lead and finally Judi came over to me and told me to feel how wet her pussy was. I fingered her for a minute and then Judi turned around. I grabbed her hips and pulled her wet hole down onto my cock. She cowgirl fucked me for a few minutes and then did the same to Wayne, followed by Alan. After Alan, she came back to me and went down the line once again in the same manner. After finishing with Alan, Judi got up and stood in front of us playing with her pussy. She said, "Okay I'm ready boys, all three of you now own this and I want it filled with every drop you have." She went straight to Wayne and slid her tongue into his mouth, while grabbing my cock and Alan's cock with each hand. She stroked us while kissing Wayne and he was fingering her. She then pushed Wayne onto his back and she was riding him in seconds. As she straddled Wayne, I got up and knelt in front of her along with Alan. We both held our cocks in front of her face as she rode Wayne. She alternated sucking our cocks and massaging our sacks with one hand at a time as she fucked Wayne.

Wayne was looking up watching her suck our cocks and holding onto her tits. After a few minutes, she got off of Wayne's cock and sat on his face. She was grinding her pussy all over his face while still working me and Alan. I started kissing her and she was moaning heavily. I told Alan to kiss her, while I sucked on her nipples, and, about a minute later, Judi came on Wayne's face. She was shaking and I knew it was a strong one. She then rolled off of Wayne and told us to lie next to each other on the bed. We did what she said, with Wayne in the middle. Judi straddled Wayne in a 69 position while Alan and I watched Wayne enjoying eating her. Judi was sucking Wayne's cock and stroking me and Alan with each hand.

At one point, Judi said, "Lick my ass, baby!" and Wayne quickly moved his tongue up to her tight little hole as told. She now had us all licking her ass! After about ten minutes, Judi got off of Wayne and said that she needed her cocks. She laid down on her back and I got on top of her first. I pounded her as Wayne got his cock sucked and she stroked Alan. I was focused at how wet her pussy was and she didn't even have any cum in it yet. I couldn't hold out any longer and I filled her with the first load. I pulled out and asked who was next, and Wayne gave Alan the nod. Alan took my place and he was fucking her gently. I commented to him if he could believe how wet she was and Alan said, "Yeah, and I can feel your cum in there too."

Judi was still busy sucking Wayne's cock and I was just lying next to her watching. Alan got up to his knees and began teasing her clit with his fingers, as he pumped her slowly. I started pinching her nipples when she had her second orgasm. Alan then started picking up the pace and he let out a grunt as he released the second load into her. Alan then pulled out and joked to Wayne that he didn't think he would need any lube. Wayne took Alan's place and started pounding away. Judi was moaning and saying, "Oh my God, I love my cocks so much!"

Judi grabbed Wayne's ass and was pulling him into her with each thrust. After a few minutes, Judi said to Wayne, "I'm so happy I own your cock now, I promise that I will keep it happy." And with that, Wayne gave Judi her third load of cum. Judi had her eyes closed and was just moaning and smiling. Alan and I were lying next to her, caressing her body as she finished fucking Wayne. Wayne pulled out and Judi told me that she wanted to taste some of our cum. I went down between her legs and placed my tongue at the bottom of her slit. It looked like a milkshake oozing out of her and I scooped up a good puddle and went up to give her a taste. Judi sucked on my tongue as I held it out for her. She moaned in approval and told Alan to start cleaning her. Alan turned her onto her side, spreading her legs wide, as he licked her pussy and ass. I could tell from her reaction when Alan made contact with her asshole. Let me just say that there is no doubt whatsoever that she really did like having her ass licked! After about five minutes, she told Alan to let Wayne get in there before it was all gone. Alan got up and Wayne went down to finish the job. Wayne sucked, licked and kissed her pussy as he clearly enjoyed the pussy that he now owned a third of.

Afterwards, Judi laid on her side behind Alan and told Wayne to hold her from behind. Wayne got in behind her and wrapped an arm and leg around her. I was now lying next to Alan, and Judi was rubbing my chest with her hand as she stretched her arm over Alan. She also had a leg wrapped over Alan and was rubbing her foot up and down my leg. I had to laugh to myself as I knew that Judi was loving cuddling with her two lovers and husband.

We laid there for about ten minutes in silence. I broke the silence by saying that I thought Judi deserved a good massage after doing such a good job on us, and Judi said, "Ooh, that sounds good." We then had Judi lie on her stomach and we surrounded her. We all started massaging her from head to toe, not missing an inch of her body. Judi was in Heaven. She kept saying that, "This feels so damn good!" and told us that this is definitely going to be a requirement when we all get together, which we all laughed at. Wayne then said that he had to get going, and Judi gave him a big kiss and thanked him. After he left, Judi asked Alan if he wanted to sleep over. Alan agreed and she told us that she was okay if either of us wanted to fuck her during the night, and not to worry about waking her up. We fell asleep with Judi in the middle and Alan was behind her. I woke up at one point to hearing Judi moaning.

Alan was fucking her from behind and after he was done, I turned Judi around and I then fucked her from behind. I wasn't sure if Alan fucked her after that, but I was done. I woke up to Judi sucking Alan's cock, but he was fucked out as well. Alan left and we took a shower together. Judi and I talked about our night over a cup of coffee.

I asked her if she was enjoying having me and her two lovers at her disposal.

And she said, "Let me ask you something, Jerry," and she explained if you could fuck me, your boss, who you've been attracted to longer than you've been married, and another good looking girl whenever you wanted, and as much as you wanted, and you could have unprotected sex with one, two or all three at the same time if you felt like it, and all three were sexually dedicated to you, and most importantly your wife truly wanted you to have that, would you be happy?

I laughed and said, "I would be in Heaven." Judi smiled and told me that I just answered my own question. Judi then asked me if I thought she asked too much by saying they had to commit to her for six months. I didn't think it was too much to ask, and let her know that I thought it would probably be amazing and that I will make a prediction that it won't end after six months. She was happy to hear me predict it wouldn't end!

I mentioned to her that she literally had live sperm swimming around inside of her every single day for about the past month and a half, minus her period days, and wondered if she ever thought about the small possibility of getting pregnant, since the pill is like 99% effective. Judi said that she had thought about it and if she did get pregnant, we would have to have a serious talk. I already knew her real answer, since I knew that she is against abortions. I told her that I would want her to keep it no matter what, which she was very happy to hear. She said that she would of course hope that it was mine, but if it wasn't, her second choice would be that it was Wayne's. She even told me that she had already thought about what a child with him would look like. I didn't respond to her, but knowing her as well as I do, and also knowing that there were feelings there, I knew that simple comment meant she had an inner desire to have a child with him, but wouldn't come out and say it. She then told me that she wants to take a day off from fucking today and I told her that I was more than fine with that, but reminded her of her promise to Wayne and Alan. She gave me a big smile and then we got ready for work.

I was thinking about our conversation from that morning all day long, and decided that I would ask Judi if she would want to try and have a child after our six month deal with Wayne and Alan was over. Well, at dinner that night, I asked Judi, but she was hesitant. She didn't say no, but she said she wanted to talk about it in six months and see how we felt. I already anticipated that this might be her answer, and I already had an idea of how to deal with it from thinking about it all day long. I explained to Judi that maybe we could talk to Wayne about it, and ask him if he would be willing to try and impregnate her along with me. That certainly got her attention! She said, "Stop fucking around Jerry, we are talking about having a child!"

I let her know that I was serious and really wanted to do it. I explained that if it wasn't mine at first, I would just want to definitely have our own child the second time. She couldn't believe that I would actually take it that far and was saying, "You're talking about me having a baby with another man!"

I responded that I wanted to hear the truth from her. I asked her straight out if she was trying to say that she wouldn't want to have Wayne's baby. She thought for a minute and her answer was, "The truth would be, if it happened by chance, I would keep it and be happy to have his child."

I then said, "So let's give Wayne the chance. I want us both to try and get you pregnant together." She stared at me for like three or four minutes in silence and then asked, "And, if it's his, then we would definitely have our own the second time?"

I said, "Yup!"

And Judi said, "Tell me more." I knew that was just as good as a yes. I told her that I was certain that Wayne would jump at the opportunity to plant his seed in her and give us his child and asked her what she thought. She said, "I think he would love to."

We talked about everything that would be involved and she said that if we did it, we would have to have a DNA test done to know whose baby it was. I agreed that we would definitely have to do that. She also said that if we did it, she would insist that we would always have to fuck her together, not separately, and she wanted me to cum in her first every time because she would prefer my child first. I really liked that she said that and asked her again if we were on for this after the six months and she said, "I'm still thinking." Judi then asked, "Let me ask you a question and I want the truth from you this time."

I of course said okay and she posed the question of what I would say if the first child turned out to be ours, and she wanted to definitely have Wayne's child second. I asked if she meant that she would only have sex with him until she got pregnant with his baby and she said, "That's exactly what I'm saying, no doubt that it would be his and you would have to watch him fuck me every single time until I was sure that I was pregnant with his child."

My answer was that I will not only watch it, but video tape it every time. I would want blow jobs in the meantime and I would get to name their baby. I also added that she would only have the one baby with him, at least on purpose, and if we had any more children than that, they would only be ours. Judi said, "Holy shit Jerry, I really do love you. That's what I want then, I'm going to have both your babies!"

She said that we needed to talk to Wayne and texted him if to come over. He answered right back that he would be over in about fifteen minutes. I kidded with her that he probably thinks that she wants to fuck him. We both laughed and she said that she was really hoping to take the day off.

Wayne came over and we sat on the couch to have our talk. I started it off by telling Wayne that I wanted him to be a permanent part of our sex life. He explained that he really liked our arrangement and that he really loved having sex with Judi. I told him that it was my idea and Judi really liked the idea and hoped that he would agree. Wayne said, "How could I say no?"

We told him that we were happy to hear that, and Judi then asked me if I wanted to tell Wayne about my other idea or should she? I told her that I wanted her to tell him. Judi then laid out our plan to Wayne about having children and described in detail how it would be done. She said after our six month deal is over, she would go off birth control so that Wayne and I could both "mate" her together. I would always get to cum in her first and then we would have a DNA test to prove whose baby it was. Whichever one of us didn't get her pregnant with the first child, they would exclusively have sex with her after the first baby was born until she knew for sure that she was pregnant again. She explained that we talked it over in detail and we would both like for him to give her a child. The only question was that we would basically compete to give her the first baby, but either way we were both going to give her a child. Wayne said that he was honored to be asked to do this and would love to do it with us. His only question was how his child would be raised. We explained that we would raise it as our own and it would be like we just decided to use a sperm donor.

We figured we would explain it later in life that we couldn't get pregnant together, so we used a sperm donor. Judi went on to explain that if the first child was mine, she wanted me to watch her get fucked by Wayne every time until she got pregnant with the second child and that I would also get to name her and Wayne's child. If the first child was Wayne's, then she would want him to watch her get fucked by me every time until she was pregnant with the second child. She assured him that she would give him as many blow jobs as he wanted during that time and that he would get to name our child. Wayne said, "Boy, you guys really thought this all out, why don't we just start right now?"

We explained that we already decided we wanted to enjoy the four of us for the next six months as we agreed on. Wayne was fine with that and joked that he was going to take a lot of vitamins for the next six months so he could knock Judi up first! I joked with him that I was getting a head start by getting to cum first every time, and I was twenty years younger, so I liked my odds better for the first one. We all laughed about it, and Judi told Wayne that she preferred that the first child was mine, but she loved the thought of having us both mating her for real at the same time and letting the strongest sperm decide who gives her our first child.

I got rock hard just hearing her say that to him! She also told us that she will be completely submissive to us when doing it. Her only demand was that she would not have sex unless it was with both of us together and we didn't clean up our cum afterwards. She explained that she wanted us to control her and mate her like it was her only purpose in life. She wanted to be told what to do, how to do it, and what position to be in. She said, "If you want me to get you a beer and hold it for you while you fuck me, then tell me to do it and I will."

I asked her what the order would be if either of us wanted to go a second or third time, and she said, "I just want to be mated by both of you, and Jerry cums first each time. After that, I don't care how many times or what the order is. Just empty everything you got in me and we will see what happens." She mentioned to Wayne that this was my idea and she wished I told her about this before she made the deal for six months, as she wouldn't have made the deal!

Wayne said that he was already hard just thinking about it and couldn't wait. Judi looked at me and asked if I was hard too, which I assured her I was. She said, "Okay, well I'm wet so let's get this over with quickly tonight." She then proceeded to stand up, take her sweatpants and thong off, put her hands on the wall and she bent over with her legs spread. Wayne got up and fucked her from behind with his pants around his ankles, as I took my pants off. Judi was yelling out, "Give me a baby, Wayne!" while he was fucking her and he came in about a minute. I got behind her and started fucking her cum-filled box while she was telling me, "That's it, push his cum deeper, I want it, I want it!" I shot my load before she got another word out! I pulled out and Judi just stayed there wiping our cum from her pussy and licking her fingers.

After a few minutes, she put her thong back on and said, "Oh, yeah, I can't wait to do this for real." After Wayne left, Judi marked down the date when the six months was to be up on the calendar hanging on the fridge. She wrote, "Baby time," with a big smiley face. I said so much for taking the night off and she gave me her devilish smile. She said, "I really need to cum right now, so I hope you can go again." I said that I was sure she could get me going again and she did just that.

Now that I made her cum and she drained me completely, she fell asleep and I was sitting there writing about our experiences. It made me realize how crazy things have gotten. It was weird, but as I go over everything step by step in writing this, I realize that we have done so much crazy stuff from when I was watching her playing pool when were on vacation. I'm also well aware that the vast majority of people would think I am nuts for allowing my wife to have a child with another man, but all I can say is that it works for us and that's all that matters to me. To me it's simple, if it makes my wife happy then it makes me happy. There is, of course, negotiation and compromise involved with most things, but I can assure you that we both have never been happier than we now are.

From where we started to where we are now, you can see from what I wrote that some things have changed like most things in life change. I originally didn't want Judi to get emotionally involved with anyone she was with, but the circumstances with Wayne changed that, and I am happy with how we accepted it and dealt with it. At first, I also wanted to have control to stop it at any time if I wanted. At that point, we have found that this lifestyle is who we are and neither of us has any intentions of stopping anything, but rather simply enjoying our chosen lifestyle.

As far as cuckolding is concerned, I have read up on it and it seems like we are on the lighter side of what is out there, but my guess is that Judi has other plans for Wayne. When I tell you that she loved doing it, I mean she really loved it and I've since noticed that she was pushing the boundaries to see how far she could take it. The funny thing to me is that we all knew that she was doing it to us, but we couldn't help it. None of us knew it before, but Judi definitely taught us to be cuckolded. Speaking for myself, I definitely wouldn't let just any woman cuckold me.

We have had so many experiences that I couldn't possibly describe every one. I did my very best in describing what I could remember the best, but every experience was great except for the one that I explained with that guy she met up with. The thing that stands out the most for me is that before we started doing this, Judi was usually submissive to me with sex and always a pleaser. Now she is clearly dominant to me with sex, but being a pleaser hasn't changed one bit. It just happens to be that she now pleases me, Wayne and Alan. She is also extremely dominant to Wayne and Alan, as I explained before. I honestly don't even know how many times Judi has gotten fucked over those three months or so, but my guess would be between 150 to 200 times! Like I said, boy did I get what I asked for!

I showed Judi the swinging lifestyle, and all the couples out there, but she didn't open up on the swinging together with another couple idea. I'm not complaining though, If it happens then great, if not, still great! The best response I got was, "Maybe one day, we'll see."

When I pressed her a little bit, she quickly shut me down and reminded me that I am not allowed to fuck any other women. The bottom line is that she is happy with what she now has. Since we started doing this, I found that I loved it and then it just became a normal part of our marriage. We both loved the dynamic of having the three of us constantly servicing her. It may sound weird, but she has a self-confidence about her that she never had before we did this. Honestly, I had never seen her happier since we met and, since we started doing this, she is always in a great mood. She was constantly telling me how much she loves me and thanking me for talking her into being a hot wife or as she likes to call it, "a married slut."

She mentioned that she primarily started doing this for me, but now she does it because she loves it. I'm just happy that she feels that way now, and I'm curious to see how much she will be able to handle it all. I'm figuring that she might be getting fucked like ten times a week or more now that Wayne and Alan can have her as they please! I just hope that it's not too much for her.

One thing I didn't mention was that Judi was constantly ordering sexy lingerie. I'm sure the UPS guy is wondering what's going on! It seemed like there was new package on our doorstep every other day from either Victoria's Secret, Fredericks, Spicy Lingerie or Venus! Everything from the assortment of nighties, to dozens of thongs, to crotchless thongs, to dozens of g-strings, to probably fifteen to twenty negligees, to skin tight spandex shorts, to sexy bras, to these fishnet body suits, to high heels, to sexy dresses, to high leather boots, and stuff like that. Some of the new underwear had so many straps or strings that it takes her five minutes just to figure out how to get one on! She even bought a thick leather choke collar that says, "Slut" on it in fake diamonds, which she likes to wear sometimes when fucking. I love when she wears it and I actually make her wear it with nothing else on but a thong or g-string, and have her walk around all day long like that when we are home on a weekend.

All I have to do is say, "Put the collar on today," and then she asks me to pick out what underwear I want her in. I didn't mention it, but both Alan and Wayne love when she wears it too. When I asked her about all this stuff that she was buying, she told me that since we started doing this, she feels sexier than she ever has in her life. She said she really enjoys wearing stuff like that for me, Alan and Wayne, and also having me pick out the outfits for her to wear for then both. Before we started doing this, she had mostly regular underwear with a handful of regular cotton thongs, one nightie that she always wore to bed, I think two negligees that she wore on our honeymoon, but that's about it. She must have spent at least two thousand dollars on all the stuff she has now.

Trust me, I'm not complaining though, and then, since Wayne was going to give her an allowance for buying lingerie, I could not have been happier. She dresses in something sexy almost every night when coming to bed now, and I love that she is wearing these really sexy thongs and g-strings almost every single day! It's like she's a different woman!

Almost every morning, she holds up two pairs of underwear and asks which one I want her to wear that day, which I happen to love doing. She always showed me that she loved me, but now we are so much tighter in more ways than we ever were, and our sex life is nothing short of a real life porn movie! It's been an amazing journey for both of us so far, and we have only just started.

The only person in our circle of friends and family who knows about our sex life is Judi's mother. They are like best friends and I have personally listened to several of their conversations while Judi was talking to her mother when we were in our car. Her mother is actually jealous of her, and always wants to hear about what we are doing. I know Judi doesn't tell her every detail, but I can tell you for a fact that she likes telling her mother about our trysts. If you ever heard her talking to her mother you would know what I mean. She told me that her mother gets off on hearing about what we do. She teases her mother for little bit by pretending that she doesn't want to tell her, until her mother is just about begging to hear about what we did. The best one I've heard was when Judi was telling her that she made me eat Alan's cum out of her. Her mother had no idea that Judi had her on speaker and she said, "Oh my God, did he like it?"

Judi told her that I love doing it and I love feeding it to her so we can kiss and taste it together. All I heard was her mother moaning on the phone! Judi went on telling her that she also makes Alan lick my cum out of her, which her mother responded, "Jesus Judi, what's your secret?" Judi smiled at me and told her that she just needed to find a husband like me, which I always think about, by the way, and she went on to tell her mother that guys like it more than she would think.

Her mother was saying, "Oooh, I don't know Judi," and Judi was laughing at her just saying that you're going to have to trust me on this one, mom. Her mother said, "Well, I don't think your father would do that." Judi agreed with her and explained that she didn't say every guy would, but there are more than she would think. I wish I could talk to some of my friends about what we do, but I know every one of my friends has said that Judi is hot and I'm sure if they knew what we did, they would be asking if they could fuck her too.

And to prove Judi's point, I am equally as sure that they would eat my cum out of her if they could fuck her afterwards! I think saying something to any of them would only lead to bad judgments and degrading comments though. So I am glad to at least be able to share our secret sex life here, and I have to say that it actually feels pretty good to tell our story to others who could at least appreciate our choice to enjoy a sexual lifestyle that differs from the normal.

I've heard the expression, "Happy Wife, Happy Life", but I changed that in my case to be, "Wife's pussy happy, very happy life." That's about it for now, but I'm sure we will have some great stories to tell in about another seven or eight months from now. I will definitely write a follow up on how it all goes.

Chapter Twenty-Two

The One Condition

"It's a deal. You get to fuck my wife. All night. But on one condition."

"Name it," Alan said, his hands trembling on her breasts as he realized that he was going to get what he wanted.

"I get to watch!"

Judi described it like this: Alan wasted no time. He was like a kid who thought that something was going to be taken away at any minute, that you or I might change our minds. So he bent me over the kitchen island and began to run his hands all over my body. Then he lifted my skirt and bunched it up around my waist. I felt the cool air on my legs, then on my ass as he pulled down my panties and tossed them aside. I heard the hiss of his zipper as he undid his jeans and pulled them down, and then kicked them aside. I dared not turn around, I was still a little in shock from this turn of events.

There I was, naked from the waist down. Alan was preparing to put his cock inside me, one hand on my hip and the other guiding his cock into position ... and my husband was watching! "For a moment I had forgotten about you," she said.

I looked over to where you were standing, wondering what I would see in your eyes. It was lust, pure lust. You were watching your best friend getting ready to fuck your wife, and I could see through your shorts that you were hard as a rock. And then I gasped, because Alan pushed himself into me in one smooth movement, all the way to the balls. I gripped the counter top with the shock of it. Alan was about the same size as you, but maybe a bit thicker. Thank goodness my pussy was already wet, because he didn't ease in slowly. He stayed still for a moment, savoring the heat and feel of my pussy. And then he began to move, getting a feel for my body. My body rocked back and forth on the counter top. And then he went faster. Harder. Deeper. I gripped the edge of the countertop to steady myself from this hot, exquisite onslaught. I was so wet, so turned on.

The vegetables on the countertop scattered everywhere as I tried to steady myself from the pounding, but I didn't care. The feeling was so hot, so wrong, and so damn good at the same time. I was getting fucked in my own kitchen by my husband's best friend! And all the while, my husband was watching us. Incredible! "Ohhh!"

Was that me who had cried out? Was that me making such wild noises? My orgasm smashed into me the same time that Alan stiffened and made a soft roaring sound, grabbing my shoulder with one of his hands and jamming himself into me as far as he could while his cock spurted cum deep into my pussy.

His hips thrashed against me as he pulsed, spurted, emptied himself. Eventually his body stilled, and he leaned over against me. His cock softened and shrank out of me. He stood up shakily, and I tried to do the same, but you stopped me. "No, stay there. I want to see," you said.

I looked over my shoulder and saw you staring at my pussy, at Alan's cum dripping out of my pussy. You were stroking your cock through your shorts as you gazed at the sight. Eventually I stood up and faced the two of you. You were more aroused than I had seen you in years. Alan was a little shaky, sitting in one of the kitchen chairs.

We were all silent, not knowing what to say or do next. It was Alan who broke the silence, "The deal was for all night, but I need a bit of help for round two," he said. His cock was limp. He looked at his cock, and then at me, "I've always been wondering what those lips of yours would feel like," he said pointedly. I looked at you for confirmation, and you nodded. I went to the chair and knelt before it, took Alan's cock in my mouth, and began to lick, suck, and taste him … his cum and my juices. He began to grow stiff again, lengthen.

His hands came up and gripped my head, holding me in place. He began to groan, "Hey, buddy, let's share this experience," Alan said to you, "if you don't mind seconds," he laughed. I couldn't turn my head to see your face, because Alan was holding me in place as I sucked his cock. But I could imagine the lust in your eyes as you stripped off your shorts and knelt behind me. My pussy was wide open to you as I knelt in front of Alan and sucked him. My pussy was glistening with Alan's cum as you put your cock into me and began to fuck me. The feeling, the experience was incredible. I had never done this before. I was sucking one man while another was fucking me from behind. Both of you were making wild animalistic sounds, and so was I.

The kitchen was filled with the sounds of passion as we all worked our way upward, each to our own climax. You were the one to cum first. You had been so aroused that you were near the edge before you put your cock into me. You let out a loud moan, and released your cum into me. "That's it, buddy!" gasped Alan, approaching his own release, "fill that hot pussy up!"

And that's exactly what you did, your hips banging hard into me as your cock spurted. I was already full of Alan's cum, so your juices were leaking out of me and running down my thighs. I was moaning and crying out, but Alan's cock was in my mouth, so it was muffled as I sucked him toward climax. And he reached it moments later, filling my mouth with his next load. Hot, sticky, salty. Pulse, spurt, pulse. I swallowed as best I could, savoring the taste of him and the excitement of the situation. I ran my tongue on the underside of his cock, milking the last drop from him until he couldn't stand it anymore and pulled out of my mouth.

We all were limp. You and I collapsed on the floor, Alan was gasping in the kitchen chair. Eventually our breathing returned to normal. And I wondered what was next. Alan had said all night. "How about you finish fixing that supper you were working on?" Alan chuckled, "we're all going to need our strength."

It was a good thing that I had begun to cook dinner, because we did indeed need our strength that night. But let me continue ... I got to my feet and felt your cum and Alan's running down my leg. I could taste Alan's cum in my mouth. The evening all seemed so unreal, like a dream. Was this all really happening? I grabbed a towel to clean myself but Alan's voice stopped me. "No," he said, "don't clean up. I want to see our cum on your legs. And don't get dressed either. I want you naked."

I looked at you and you nodded, looking as dazed as me at this turn of events. But I also saw lust in your eyes. You liked watching Alan fuck me. You liked watching me suck him as you fucked me from behind. This all had to be a dream. I cooked dinner completely naked. I could feel your eyes and Alan's eyes watching my body as I worked. I could almost feel the heat of your stares on me as I cooked, working on autopilot. Soon your stares began to affect me, along with the feel of the wet sticky cum on my thighs.

Autopilot shut down and arousal kicked in. I began to move my hips provocatively as I worked. I would lean over the counter more than I had to in order to reach a spice, my ass displayed for both of you to enjoy. After about ten minutes of this, I slipped the casserole into the oven and glanced over my shoulder. Both of you were staring at me in lust, stroking your cocks as you watched my body move. The sight of your two hard cocks was electrifying for me. I managed my most sultry look and slowly sat back and laid down on the lower part of the kitchen island. It was the perfect height, although I had to prop myself up on my elbows since it was so narrow. "Anybody want an appetizer before dinner?" I managed, amazed at my boldness.

You jumped up, but Alan stopped you. "Hey, she's mine tonight, not yours," and you reluctantly backed off. I can't remember the last time I had seen you that aroused. Your cock was so big and hard, I could tell it was painful. Alan walked up to the counter, still stroking his cock. I thought he was going to fuck me again, and my pussy was wet, waiting for him. But, to my surprise, he put his strong arms under my hips and legs, and lowered his mouth to my pussy, inhaling my scent. "Mmm, I do love a good cream pie," he said, and ran his tongue from my pussy to my clit. I gasped, not believing he was eating my pussy when it was so full of cum.

He pressed his lips against me and began to taste and explore. I groaned and arched my back against him, and soon my hands were tangling in his hair, pulling him closer. The feeling was incredible! I had a fleeting thought of what you were thinking seeing me like this, but the thought fled as my orgasm began to build. Alan pushed me higher toward the brink, his mouth sucking on my clit as his fingers worked inside of me. The brink came with a scream.

Was that me screaming? I could feel myself flying, falling as I had the most shattering orgasm I think I've ever had. I shook, I shuddered, I held onto Alan's hair for dear life as I came and came, and came again, over and over. Eventually my body went limp and Alan was gone. When had he stood up? I opened my eyes and saw him standing there over me. Looking pleased. Looking possessive. Looking like he was not done with me yet from the look of his hard cock.

I looked around for you and saw you right where you were before, a glazed lustful look in your eyes, still stroking your cock. You obviously liked what you were watching. As I said, Alan was not done with me yet, not by a long shot! As I lay there trying to recover, he stepped forward and pulled me to the edge of the counter. He slowly, deliberately spread my legs apart, reached down and wrapped his arms around my thighs, and slowly pulled me and my pussy onto his hard cock. I gasped as his cock filled my pussy for the second time that night. He adjusted his position, holding me in place with his arms around my thighs. I was aware that I couldn't have moved away or escaped him, as he held me locked in place on his cock, not that I wanted to escape. He began to move. Slowly at first, pulling out to the tip of his cock, then slowly burying himself deep up to this balls. The rhythm increased. Faster. Deeper. Harder, until he was slapping himself into me in a hard and fast rhythm that had me moaning and gasping. He had cum twice already, so he was not going to cum really quickly this third time. He was going to be fucking me like this for awhile until he came. And then fucking me some more all night. I was dimly aware that my pussy was going to be sore tomorrow, but I didn't care. This felt too fucking good to offer any protest.

"Jerry," Alan said, his voice ragged as he pumped deeply into me, "I think that sexy mouth of hers needs some attention." I had frankly forgotten about you. I looked over to where you were, but you had moved already. You were standing at the other side of the counter behind me. You eased me onto my back onto the counter. I had been propped up on my elbows before this. Alan never missed a bit of rhythm as he continued to fuck me. The counter was narrow, so my head hung off the end, my neck bent backward. My mouth opened for you, and you slid your cock past my lips, into my mouth, my throat. I had been deep throating you for years, but never from this position. You definitely got the feel you wanted, not wanting to choke me. Your rhythm increased until you two were in perfect rhythm with each other.

Words can't express the sensation of being fucked from both ends at the same time, Alan in my pussy, and you in my mouth. It was different from when I was in the doggie position. I had some freedom of movement in that position. But now I was on my back, completely helpless to the onslaught. I braced myself against the edge of the counter as both of you fucked me in perfect synchronous time. I could hear both of you groan as you worked toward your peak. Alan came first, gripping my hips even tighter as he spurted and spasmed and filled me with his cum again. Soon I could hear your breathing grow ragged as you neared your own climax, "Oh baby, oh baby, ohhh shit!" you cried out as you begin to cum.

I have always loved the taste of your cum. I swallow eagerly, but found that I couldn't keep up in this upside down position. Your cum dribbled out of the corner of my mouth, dribbling down my face and into my hair as you shook and pulsed and filled my mouth beyond capacity. I sucked and licked and drained you until you couldn't stand it anymore and pulled out. What a sight we must have made! I laid there limp and gasping on the counter top, cum dripping from my pussy and mouth. Both of you were leaning against the counter for support, your cocks limp and glistening with your cum and my juices.

Gradually our breathing returned to normal. And the oven timer dinged. Time to refuel. Like Alan said, we're all going to need our strength.

Made in the USA
Columbia, SC
23 February 2018